LUNA STATION
QUARTERLY

Issue 040 | December 2019

The Potions & Poisons Issue

Editor-in-Chief

Jennifer Lyn Parsons

Editors

Rocky Breen • Linda Codega • Angelica Fyfe
Shel Graves • Cathrin Hagey • Sarah McGill
Cait Ryan • Carly Racklin • Shanna Ross
Tamara Lee Rutledge • Gô Shoemake • Margaret Stewart

LUNA STATION PRESS
NEW JERSEY

First Paperback Edition December 2019
ISBN: 978-1-949077-13-1

Luna Station Quarterly publishes short fiction on March 1st, June 1st,
September 1st, and December 1st. For more information and submission
guidelines, please visit our website at lunastationquarterly.com

For Luna Station Press

Creative Director - Tara Quinn Lindsey
Editor-in-Chief & Founder - Jennifer Lyn Parsons

LUNA STATION PRESS

www.lunastationpress.com

CONTENTS

Editorial

Tara Quinn Lindsey

Tara Quinn Lindsey is a poet & essayist. Her books include *The Esbat Sequence, sQuallor//gLamour, Invisible Compositions* & *Bedtime Stories For Insouciant Alchemists*. To learn more, visit her at taralindsey.com

PLACE-HOLDER

PLACE-
HOLDER

PLACE-
HOLDER

PLACE-HOLDER

LSQ | 040

All Manner of Wounds

Emily Strempler

Emily Strempler lives and writes in Banff National Park, in the beautiful Canadian Rockies. You can find her on instagram (@estrempler).

"...Okay, but after that..." Her voice was soft and clear, filtered through the speaker of the phone pressed between Noemi's shoulder and ear.

"I have work..." Dark curtains shrouded the room's small window. A table lamp sat on the floor beside a mattress heaped with blankets. In the dim light, Noemi sat cross legged, a tray of medical supplies balanced on the pillow beside her. She had her t-shirt pulled half-off. Her body was covered in tattoos, band-aids scattered across a few bare patches on her stomach and thighs. "...Eleven, probably..." She unscrewed the top of a glass vial with an alcohol wipe. Setting the lid on an empty part of the tray, she shifted the phone against her ear and picked up a syringe. "...Yeah, I'll come by, but I can't stay up forever..." Dipping the syringe, she measured out a dose and drew the medicine from the bottle. Setting the vial on the tray, she used another alcohol wipe to screw the lid back on. "Yeah...Me too...Look, I'm sorry...I've got to run..." She folded it over and swabbed a patch of skin on her stomach. "You too," she made a kissing noise, then laughed, "Bye..."

She waited for the chime of the call to go dead before shifting the phone back off her shoulder. It landed among the blankets, its display casting a glow across the folds behind her. Pinching an inch of skin between her fingers, she inserted the needle carefully, injecting the contents of the syringe into the layer of fat under her skin. There was a light knock on the door. "Mom..."

"Yes?" She withdrew the needle. Pulling a band aid from an open package on the tray, she peeled off the paper and stuck it down over the site, blotting out a small drop of blood.

"Gramma wants to know if you want breakfast."

"I would love breakfast, but tell Gramma I'll be a minute, and I have to run out right after, okay?"

"Yeah, okay, I'll tell her..."

***

The apartment was small, kitchen, dining, and living rooms packed together, with a counter and a change of flooring in between. The couch was folded down into a bed. Mismatched shelving lined the walls, stacked with boxes and bins, canning jars, and aging medical texts. The windows were covered by blackout curtains.

Noemi's mother stood at the stove in a kitchen full of lab equipment. A centrifuge spun on the table, plugged into a large portable battery. Three plates were lined up on the counter beside her, ready with slices of dense, whole wheat bread and cut fruit. She doled out eggs from a frying pan and put it back on the burner, switching off the heat.

Noemi reached for a plate. Her hand was blocked with a swish of her mother's spatula. "You took your insulin?"

"Ten minutes ago."

Withdrawing the spatula, she let Noemi take a plate. "You should look at your daughter's homework before you leave."

"I looked at it last night. It's fine."

"Is it? It looked all wrong to me."

"That's how they're supposed to do it now. The teacher can see their calculator history, so they don't need to copy it down anymore."

"Well, she's your daughter..."

Noemi kissed her cheek. "Thank you for making breakfast. This looks great."

***

Outside the apartment complex, it was a shadowy dawn. The area had once been prime real estate, less than a block from the waterfront. Rows of stately townhouses lined the street, their interiors subdivided into cheap rentals. At the end of the road, the seawall loomed, three towering stories of reinforced concrete. Raised sidewalks and roadbeds ran over a vast system of concrete pillars and steel supports, stretching to meet the wall at its upper edge. Faint sunlight slanted down through the rain grates far overhead.

Noemi walked along the road, backpack slung over her shoulder. Traffic passed at a crawl. Taking a turn past a row of commercial storefronts, she entered the small ground floor office of a bank, and stepped into the elevator. On the other side, the doors opened into a sunlight flooded lobby. Pulling up a car service on her phone as she walked, she requested a ride and stopped at the corner to wait.

The sidewalks were packed with people. Cars streamed past each other, weaving in and out with computerized efficiency. Across the street, a group of tourists posed for a photo in front of a large, glass art installation designed to look like a miniature version of the city skyline.

A dinged up beige conversion pulled up. Noemi squeezed in with the two already in the back seat. Leaning against the window with her bag in her lap, she checked her predicted ride time. Ten minutes. She began to scroll down through the itinerary. The time ticked down for a few seconds, then, as the car took a turn, it flipped to thirty without adding another passenger. They turned again and it flipped back. Noemi tilted her screen toward the man sitting beside her, "Is this your stop moving up and down the list?"

"Oh...Not mine."

She leaned forward, showing it to the couple in the front seats. They squinted at the screen. "Oh god, this happened last time, too..." The woman said, already looking at her phone, "It wants someone to pay for priority."

"I don't think that's legal."

"Probably not, right?" She had the service open on her phone. "I bet it stops in a year or two. You know, once they get sued, again. It was them that got sued a while back, right?" She looked at the man beside her, who shrugged. "I think it was them. They paid a fine. Something to do with inaccurate ride times..." She tapped an option, angling the phone's camera toward her face to give authorization. "There! Should clear up once it refreshes."

"Thank you."

"Oh, it's no problem. Small price to pay to actually get where you're going, if you ask me..."

The ride time flipped to thirty minutes. Shifting her bag off her knees, she put her phone in a side pocket and pulled out a heavy pharmaceutical textbook and a pen. Squeezing the backpack down between her legs and the front seat, she flipped the textbook open to a bookmark. The margins were full of tiny, handwritten notes, pieces of text underlined once or twice for emphasis. The car meandered through the city, picking up and dropping off passengers. It changed its route as it went, and by the time it pulled up in front of the university, an hour had passed.

Carrying the textbook and pen, backpack slung over her shoulder, Noemi jogged up the steps, took the stairs up a couple floors, and ducked into a classroom. Taking a seat near the back, she started to unpack her things. The professor paused mid-lecture, "Miss Davis...come see me after class. I'll give you a copy of the notes you missed. You're going to want them before starting your paper next week." She nodded, flipping open her laptop, and he turned back to the class. "Now, who remembers what we were discussing?" He pointed to a young man in the front. "You."

"Drug safety and the role of ethics and law in prescription practice."

"Correct. And what does that mean to you?"

"I think they're all the same thing."

"Okay, interesting perspective there. Anyone have thoughts on that?" A few hands went up. "You...blue shirt in the third row..."

***

Noemi stuffed her bag into a locker in a long concrete hallway lit with harsh fluorescent lights. She had changed into a blue work uniform, an employee ID card clipped to her shirt on a retractable lanyard. She leaned into the locker door to close it. After a moment's silence, it locked with an automated whir. Stopping at a large touchscreen mounted by a set of steamy glass doors, she passed her card across the sensor and pulled up her shift information. She tapped the sign in button and a timer started in the top corner, counting up payable hours from zero. The doors slid open with a squeak.

The air inside was full of mist. Tinted light streamed from thousands of precisely angled lamps. The room stretched off into the distance, a perfect grid of grow racks and concrete pillars. It smelled of minerals and fertilizer. Noemi picked up a tablet by the door. It was coated in a thin layer of plastic to keep out the damp. The screen blinked a copyright and disclosure warning as she signed in. She okayed it without really looking. Flipping through several menus of diagnostic information, she pulled up a log of the day's error reports.

***

"...I just wanted to check if you still wanted me to come..." Leaning against the non-descript brick façade of the farm's surface entrance, Noemi held her phone to her ear with her shoulder, taking bites of a vending machine sandwich between sentences. The street was dark. A group of men hung around outside the door to a bar on the opposite corner. "No, you don't have to send a car, I'll grab one..." She stopped to chew. "...Yeah, of course. I thought you might be asleep by now..." Finishing off the sandwich, she crumpled up the paper package and tossed it into an overflowing trash can. "...Yeah. I'm on my way. Thirty minutes, maybe...See you then." Shifting the phone off her shoulder, she hung up the call.

Taking a side street, she headed for an old fire escape running up the side of a building a block down. It was locked up at the bottom, a scuffed painter's ladder leaning up against the wall beside it. She climbed up and over the barrier and jogged up several flights to street level. Putting in a request for a shared car, she walked until the confirmation came through.

A blue SUV pulled up to the corner a few minutes later, empty, for once, of other passengers. She kicked off her shoes in the backseat, snapped a photo of the empty car. "Might even be less than thirty minutes," she wrote, sending the picture along after it.

"Sweet."

No other requests came in for the car. Noemi let herself doze in the back. She woke with a start to the car's exasperated beeping and an overstay charge ticking up on her phone. It had overshot the front doors of the apartment tower by a block and a half. Getting out, she took another picture and sent it with the message, "Never mind."

A frowning face came back.

"I'll be five. Just walking."

"Door's open. 3651."

At the entrance, she typed in the code. The door clicked open, letting her through into a lobby decorated with smooth white tile and soft grey wallpaper. She took an empty elevator up. The apartment door was propped open with a shoe, the upbeat sound of pop music drifting out into the hall.

Noemi kicked the shoe inside. "Mila?"

"Yeah, I'm in the kitchen...Have you eaten already? I have leftovers!"

Noemi put her bag down by the door and walked into the kitchen. "I'd have to take another shot."

Mila was sitting on one end of the kitchen island, a takeout container in her lap, her curly, bottle-blonde hair pulled into twin ponytail puffs. "So? If you're hungry..." She offered the container. "It's great, but they always send too much."

"I'm good," Noemi said, "But that smells delicious."

"Take it for breakfast! I can grab something at work." Hopping down from the counter, she looked around for the container's lid. She found it under a napkin, snapped it on, and put the container in the fridge.

"How was your day?"

"Better now that you're here," Mila said, wrapping her arms around Noemi's neck and pulling her into a kiss. "God! I'm so tired. I drank two cups of coffee just so I could stay up." She laughed. "You look great, by the way. I like your work uniform. It's real repair-man chic."

"I can change. I'm pretty sure it's dirty, anyway."

"Don't, I like it..."

***

The bedroom was dark and quiet. Lying awake, Mila held Noemi close against her chest, long hair tickling her face. It was late, and through the thin veil of airy curtains, she could see the lights of a sleepy skyline. "Emmy..."

"Hmm?"

"Are you still awake?"

"No..."

Mila settled back in, her mouth and nose resting against the back of Noemi's head. "Don't you sometimes feel, like...I don't know... Like maybe we should know each other better?"

"Hmm?"

"I don't even know where you live..."

"Your place is nicer..." Noemi mumbled.

"So?"

"Is it important?" she said.

"I don't know...sometimes I just feel like...like we've been dating a long time you know...and I know hardly anything about you... like, I haven't met your parents, or your friends..."

"Can we talk about it when it isn't the middle of the night?" Rolling over, she put her arms around Mila and pressed a soft, sleepy kiss to her cheek. "I don't have a lot of time...I just want to be with you...Is that okay?"

"Yeah...I'm sorry, I was just..."

"Shh..." Noemi whispered, "It's late..."

***

Mila woke to the sing-song tones of her alarm. The side of the bed where Noemi had slept the night before had been neatly turned down, the pillow fluffed and squared off. "Off," she mumbled. The alarm kept singing along, growing in volume as it went. Picking her head up off the pillow, Mila squinted at it. "Off." It quieted, the screen winking off, as if drifting back to sleep.

A moment later it lit back up with a cheery, "Good morning!" It displayed the weather and the traffic times along her usual routes, recent headlines and notifications. The coffeemaker gurgled from the other room. Mila rolled out of bed, grabbed the phone without looking at it and turned the screen off.

Padding out to the kitchen in bare feet, she found a note tucked under a mug on the counter beside the coffeemaker.

***

Good morning beautiful,

I hope the coffee is fresh. I set the timer from your alarm, but I'm not sure I did it right. It's the thought that counts, right?

I took those leftovers for breakfast. Hoping you weren't secretly wishing I'd leave them.

We should try to make time for a proper evening out next week. I've been missing you.

Emmy

***

Mila pulled up her messages on her phone and tapped on Noemi's name. "You got the timer perfect," she wrote, then, "Sorry for being weird last night." Putting her phone down on the counter, she opened the fridge and glanced inside. She closed it again with a sigh. Pulling up a delivery service on her phone, she ordered a breakfast wrap to her office. She put the mug back in the cupboard. Filling a thermos, she took it with her back to the bedroom to get dressed.

She called herself a solo-car and sat in the back, answering emails and drinking coffee. There were protesters out front, not for her company but for one a few floors down. They were cordoned off to a small corner of the square, behind a barricade of ropes and police. Snapping a picture, she sent it off to a coworker upstairs, "What did they do this time?"

"There was a story in the Times yesterday. Some shit about child labor or something. Didn't read it."

"I thought they dealt with that?"

"Apparently not."

The elevators were packed. She looked up a knockoff of the story to avoid the paywall and skimmed it on her way up to the twentieth floor. It had nothing to do with child labor. It was about otters. She sent a link to the coworker along with a gif of a sad otter, authorized the office doors from her phone and walked down a long hallway to her glass walled office, one little cube among many, at the far end near the windows.

It was sparsely decorated, a single painting hanging on the one solid wall. A wilted little plant sat on the corner of the desk next to a framed picture of her parents' dog. Flopping into her chair, she looked up the day's schedule on her phone. Her first meeting had been pushed back an hour, so she pulled up her message thread with Noemi.

Scrolling back through their conversations, she selected a picture Noemi had sent a few weeks earlier and expanded it to fill the screen. There was a wall behind her head in the shot, a shelf with a few blurry objects on it, a box and some books. She swiped back through more pictures, sent over months: Noemi with her head resting on a patterned pillowcase, in a shared car with two sleeping strangers, at the zoo with the fluffy hair of a child in the background behind her shoulder. She swiped out of the gallery. "Do you see this ever being serious?" she wrote. She hit send and it went through, joining her other, unread, messages from earlier that morning.

There was a knock on the door.

A lanky young man in faded jeans stood in the hall, holding a paper bag and a payment tablet. Getting up from her desk, she opened the door and took the bag. He offered the tablet. "I have a card on file," she said.

"You need to reconfirm every ten orders."

"Fine, let me see that, then..." She signed on the touch screen with her finger, confirmed her account's tipping policy, and handed it back. "Here-- Thank you...Sorry, I'm just having a bit of a day."

"Yeah, sure. Don't worry about it," he said, already looking down at the tablet. "Look, if you're going to rate me, can you make it good? I had a bad customer last week and it's affecting my rating."

"Uh...Sure," Mila said, "I can do that."

***

"Do you see this ever being serious?"

Noemi's phone rested on her knee. She sat in a stall in the university washrooms, a small, insulated case open in her lap. She had a needle in her hand, a vial of insulin propped open in the case. "I don't know if I have time for something serious right now," she wrote. "I don't want to get your hopes up just to let you down."

Turning her phone off, she dropped it into her bag so she couldn't see the screen light up. She dipped the needle, then stopped to fish her phone back out of her bag. Turning the screen on, she found the note with her calculations written in it. She administered her shot. Then, she flipped back to her messages and checked to see if they had been read. They had. "I want to keep seeing you," she wrote. An error popped up. *Not delivered.* "I really like you." *Not delivered.* "Please text me back." *Not delivered.*

Noemi stared at her phone. The error messages sat, unchanging, on the screen. After a while, the screen turned off. She tapped to turn it back on. Scrolling through her options, she selected the dating service they'd met on and found Mila's profile at the top of her history. It had been deactivated.

***

Mila kicked her shoes off just inside the door to her apartment. She tossed her purse onto the kitchen counter and checked the fridge. It was empty except for a few cans of sparkling water and a handful of ketchup packets. She fished her phone out of her bag, wandered into the living room, and flopped down onto the couch. It was off. She powered it on. The screen lit up a moment later, network information popping back into the top corner. Notifications pinged in.

She selected the conversation with Noemi. "Sorry," she wrote, "My phone was off. I shouldn't have pushed you. I understand you're busy." Then, "We can keep things casual, if that's what you want."

A response came back right away. "We should talk," Noemi said. "In person, I mean." Then, "115A Lower W 47th St. 11:05pm. I'll wait outside for you. I have to turn my phone off in five. I'm at work."

Mila looked up the address. It was below street level. Some kind of warehouse. "Perfect place for a murder," she wrote back.

"You said you wanted to know where I work. There's a decent bar across the street. I thought we could grab a drink."

"Oh. Yeah. Sorry."

"It's fine."

"See you then," Mila wrote. The message went unread, so she swiped out of the conversation and selected a delivery service, putting in an order for pizza and a bottle of wine. She flicked over to the car service while she waited for it to go through and checked the drive times for the address Noemi had given her. It was off route. She switched to premium and the base rate doubled. A liability warning filled the screen. She okayed it and began scrolling through her options.

***

The car dropped Mila off on a dark street lined with industrial shop fronts. Underneath the roadway, the air was stale and dead. Fumes lingered. Cars rumbled overhead. Noemi leaned against a lamppost, one foot kicked up, backpack hanging off her shoulder. Her work shirt was unbuttoned, still tucked in, a pale tank top showing underneath. She had her phone out, her face highlighted in the glow. Mila pushed her hands down in her pockets.

Spotting her, Noemi straightened up, offering a wave and a half-smile. She walked over. When she got close, she gestured to the building behind her. "I'm working here for the next ten months, until my contract runs out."

"What is it?"

"It's a farm. They grow greens. Cabbage, kale, that kind of thing…"

"I didn't know they did farming around here."

"It's convenient for the restaurants."

"I hope you at least get hazard pay…"

Noemi laughed. "I live down here." She pointed off down the street. "Couple blocks that way."

"Oh…Sorry, I shouldn't have said…"

"It's fine," Noemi said, "How was work?"

"Oh my god, it was nothing but meetings."

"That doesn't sound so bad."

"No, you don't get it. None of them mattered at all! I don't even know why I had to be there. How am I supposed to get anything done if I'm never at my desk? I think they want me to take it home with me. As if, right?" They walked across the street to the bar, Mila following Noemi as she pushed through the crowd outside the front door.

It was up a flight of stairs and down a hallway, in the back of a building that seemed to be mostly maintenance shops and transportation company offices. The bar looked as if it hadn't changed in about fifty years. Taking a table near the back, Noemi picked up a cracked tablet off its stand and wiped it with a paper napkin before looking at the menu. "I need food," she said, jamming her thumb against the screen to get the presses to register. "Sorry, I'm just going to order this. You can take your time." It went through, and she passed the tablet across.

Mila glanced at the menu. There wasn't much, a few items of deep-fried pub food and some cheap domestic beers, most of which were sold out. "I already ate. You want a beer?"

"Sure."

She tried to enter her order, but it didn't respond.

"You have to really jab it," Noemi said, taking it back, "They just got these a couple years ago, believe it or not. I think they're knockoffs."

***

The lights of passing cars strobed through the drainage grates. It was raining, water streaming down through the gaps to pool in the street below. The air was warm. Mila leaned on Noemi, one arm slung over her shoulders, wobbly on her feet as they walked down the sidewalk toward the corner. "You should come home with me!" she said, "You have, what? School tomorrow? You have time..."

"Uh...No...I have work. It's Saturday."

"Work on Saturdays should *not* be a thing! Saturdays are for... like, watching shows in pajamas...or going to the park or whatever...That's the point. Not work!"

"Who would cook and stuff?"

"Robots! They have those, right? Cooking robots...In China or Japan or something?" Letting go of Noemi, Mila stopped walking to pull out her phone, struggling to type into the search bar. "Oh my god! I can't type anything...look...look..." She showed Noemi her screen. "What the hell is that? Like...That doesn't say robot at all..." Noemi took her phone and squinted at it. "See..."

Mila said, she wandered a few steps away, then stopped, staring up at the rain falling through the grates. The droplets were lit blue and red and gold. "Damn, that's pretty..."

Noemi took her hand. "Come on..."

"Where are we going?"

"Home. We're sneaking in...Shh..." She put a finger to her lips, then burst out laughing. "I want you to stay..." Wrapping her arms around Mila, she rested her head on her shoulder. "I really like you..."

They meandered down the street and up the stairs to the apartment. Noemi took a couple tries to open the door. A sprinkling of power lights winked away in the black shadows of the kitchen. Faint snoring came from the couch bed in the living room. Noemi pulled Mila by the hand around the furniture and clutter, into her room.

***

Mila woke to the blaring of an unfamiliar alarm. She blinked at the heavy curtains. The light leaking around them from the street was thin, tinted with reds and blues. There was shouting in the hallway. She groped in the dark for her shirt and pulled it on over her head. Sitting up in bed, she rubbed her eyes.

"...You said you wouldn't bring anyone here! Do you have any idea what kind of risk this is? For me? For your daughter? Emmy! Are you listening to me?"

"I'm taking my fucking pills. Save it."

"She needs to leave. Now!"

"Shh. You're going to wake Gabby."

"How long have you known her? Hmm? What if you can't trust her? Did you even think about that?"

"We've been dating for a long time, Mom. I know her."

"You should have asked me first!"

"I'm sorry. I was drunk. I won't do it again, okay?"

Mila crept across the room. There was an old tablet sitting propped up by the mirror, a blood sugar readout blinking bright across the screen. The alarm blared out though a set of attached speakers. A box sat open on the dresser beside it, full of bottles and plastic bagged needles, packages of alcohol wipes and glucose tablets. She picked up one of the bottles. It had a home printed label on it, details written in fine-tipped permanent marker. Tucked in next to the bottles was a little notebook packed with dosage calculations. She flipped through a few pages of scribbled numbers, then put it back.

After a while, the alarm turned itself off. The conversation outside had quieted to a murmur. Mila was still a little drunk, her head swimming as she searched the floor for her pants. She dressed, found her purse on the chair by the bed, and slipped out into the apartment, closing the door carefully behind her.

A lamp was on in the living room. In the low light, she could make out details that had been invisible to her the night before. Images floated through her head from an online special her mother had sent her a few years earlier, some investigative thing, about underground medical practices and off-market pharmaceuticals. Boxes of cellulose capsules sat open on the table beside a stack of books. Herbs steeped in large jars. There was lab equipment out on the counter, next to a row of slow cookers plugged into a portable battery.

She wandered through into the living room. "I should go."

Noemi was sitting on the edge of the folded down couch-bed in a bra and shorts, her head resting in her hand. "No," she said, "It's fine. You can sleep. It doesn't make any difference at this point." She looked up at her mother, standing next to her. "That fine?"

"No, thank you," Mila said, "I'm so sorry for disturbing you like this. It won't happen again." She pulled on her shoes and stepped out into the hall. The corridors felt like a maze in the bleary dark. Making her way out through a side door, she wandered until she found a street sign and, using that for her location, called herself a priority car.

As it wound its way to the nearest ramp, she pulled up articles about off-market and homemade insulin on her phone. She copied a few links and fired them off to Noemi. "Aren't you worried?" she wrote, "You could die."

"All the time."

"Then why? Surely there's some kind of insurance you can get for it? Isn't there a program for that?"

"I don't qualify." Then, a moment later. "Please, just don't tell anyone."

"What if something happens?"

"I don't like to think about it."

Mila rested her phone in her lap. The screen drifted and blurred. She wiped her eyes with the side of her hand and put her phone away, curling up on the seat.

***

Noemi washed her face in the bathroom sink on her five-minute break. The halls were quiet, as always, her phone out of reach in the lockers. She stared at her face in the mirror, the tiny tattooed feather on the corner of her jaw, the freckles on her forehead and cheek. She wasn't wearing any makeup. There were bags under her eyes, lines creasing the corners. Her skin looked grey under the crappy fluorescent lights. Dabbing her face dry with a paper towel, she lingered a while longer before going back to work.

It was night when she swiped off shift. She bought a sandwich from the breakroom vending machine and took a different, longer route home, to avoid retracing her steps from the night before. The neighborhood was quiet, cop cars patrolling slowly along the streets. One stopped and waved her over. She showed the woman her work ID. "Stay safe out there tonight," the officer said, "We've had a lot of calls." Noemi thanked her for the tip and kept walking, past a glaringly lit park where a group of kids were playing basketball.

She took a turn down a darkened side street lined with apartment buildings and run-down old store fronts. A few of the streetlights were burnt out. Blue and red lights bounced off the facades at a distant intersection, streaking across the pavement. Noemi's heart skipped in her chest. Ditching her backpack in a window well, she jogged to the corner.

The street in front of her building was full of police cars and caution tape. Her mind raced, visions of shootings and arrests and court cases. Her daughter going into care. There was an ambulance waiting outside. Neighbors stood in the street. The front door of the building next to hers was open. Paramedics and police moved in and out. A stretcher sat empty on the sidewalk. An officer approached her, one hand on the call button on his radio. The lens of a body camera stared at her from his chest. "Good evening, Miss," he said, "Can I help you?"

"I'm just trying to walk home."

"Well, I'd recommend taking a different route, if you can. We still have an active crime scene on our hands here. You live in the area?"

She nodded.

He pulled out a notebook and wrote down a number. "If you have any information you think might be relevant, give me a call during office hours. Or leave a message with the secretary. Either way, it'll get to me."

"What happened?"

"Afraid I'm not at liberty to say. If you don't already know, you're going to have to wait and watch it on the news like everyone else."

Noemi took the slip of paper he offered. "Sure," she said. She pointed back the way she had come. "I'm just going to head home now, if that's okay..."

"Have a wonderful night."

She pocketed the piece of paper, turning her back on the scene. Her feet felt numb. Her throat was tight. The air felt hot and oppressive around her. Wandering back down the street to the building where she had abandoned her bag, she fished it out of the window well. She sat down on the steps of the building and pulled out her phone. Selecting Mila's face in her quick access, she held it to her ear, listening as it rang, once, twice, three times.

On the fifth ring, Mila picked up. "Emmy? I thought you were at work. Oh...I guess you're off now...Look...I'm sorry for earlier..."

Noemi burst into tears, muffling them with her hand. She rocked on the steps. "Emmy? What's wrong?"

"There were police...in front of my building...when I got home... and I thought..."

"Oh god..."

"I thought you..."

"I'm so sorry! I didn't even think...Where are you? I'm coming, okay...I just wanted to get out of your mother's space, because I thought...I'm so sorry! I didn't even think about that-- Where are you? Is there an intersection...or?"

"West 43rd and 10th."

"Okay, I'm calling a car. Hang on."

"I'm sorry. I should have known you wouldn't, I just...I can't go home, with all the...It would be..."

"It's okay, Emmy, just breathe. They're okay. We can call and make sure from the car. I'm coming to get you. I'm only ten minutes away..."

Liar, Liar, Tongue on Fire

Janessa Mulepati

Janessa Mulepati lives in the northeast United States. She is a writer and artist, and believes that fiction, at its best, reminds us that every single person has a rich life, inner and outer, that we will barely come to know. Her work has appeared in PIF Magazine, Driftwood Press, and The Arcanist. Find her on Twitter @Nessi_Writes.

Perjured tongues were burning tongues—a familiar saying and reality to Pan, who sat on a bench outside the courtroom. The proceedings were a murmur to his ears, a bored hum overridden by the scuff of his shoes across the floor. A shoe nail in one heel had wiggled loose, catching stone, metal to granite with each swing of his legs.

He caught himself and stilled. His legs protested.

No fidgeting, he told them. *You know better.*

For now, he was unnoticed—anybody's servant boy in a cloak and cap—as he waited for a yay or nay so he might return home before lamplighters took to the streets. Nearby, guards crowded the courtroom doorway to better hear the judge.

"Done," one of them said. "A lefty."

The guard turned to Pan and jerked her thumb toward the courtyard.

"Your job, boy."

Left it was, out the Farewell Door and into a fenced yard where the public might watch justice delivered. The hanging platform needn't be bothered with this one, not for perjury. The walkway in front of the main gate sufficed for the man forced to kneel there. Already, a crowd had gathered, children hoisted atop shoulders so they too might gape.

Pan handed a vial to the court's hand and retreated to the edge of the walkway. The routine that followed was generations old.

A harness held the perjured man's mouth open, and pliers extended his tongue. Hands grappled. Tears flowed. The court's hand announced the man's crimes and invoked the blessing of Nicero, god of justice, while town criers ran off to spread the news.

The groundkeeper, a lanky man always lurking around the yard, stole up beside Pan with a shake of his head.

"Mark my words, boy. This one deserved it."

Pan remained silent.

"Wait until you see the next one. They reeled in a true horror. Tongue smooth as rose petals." The man snapped his fingers, drawing Pan's eyes to his. "Mark me, boy. It's coming, and you won't forget it."

Anxiety curled fingers over Pan's scalp, and the boy fixed his eyes to the walkway. He could almost ignore the sour whiff of liar acid as the vial's cork popped free, but never the screams that followed as a single drop fell from bottle to tongue.

***

The workroom smelled of lizards, a scent Pan could only describe as hay litter and scales oily with musk. Burning juniper did little to mask the stench and incited coughing when the breeze blew inward, but Pan would take coughing over the reek of bile when it came time to harvest liar acid.

A lizard studied him from inside its cage, its eyes as golden as the acid slicking its teeth. A tongue darted out to lick one eye, glossing it. It gleamed like the rosin Pan melted to protect corks when bottling liar acid.

Acid and gloss. Juniper and musk. Pan hadn't liked any of it at first, but he was an expert caretaker now and so very fortunate.

"Feathers," he told Lilac, one of the lizards. "I have a mattress with real feathers. No hay. No make-yourself-a-pallet before the older boys take all the blankets. I told you all about that. And how they stole tongs from the fireplace and made us fight."

How they'd pushed him to the back of the line whenever guests had come to size up orphans for manual labor or apprenticeships.

He smiled at Lilac. The lizards never complained about his chattering or keeping him company. Sometimes, he fancied they might thank him for the charcoal landscapes he drew for their cages, the sketches detailed down to pebbles and leaves.

Mistress swept into the room, her words brisk.

"Clean the floors. Change hay. Feed the lizards."

Pan wrote each sentence on the room's chalkboard, and would cross each one out as he completed tasks. Illiterate as he was, he'd memorized the roster of commands back when Mistress had been the one writing them down, and could rearrange the sentences at will.

"Good," Mistress said. "Very good. Handwriting says a lot about a person. Funny you slant your L's the same way. It means we're clever, according to the quill experts!"

Mistress grinned and handed him a bowl of porridge.

"Of course," the woman said. "Quill analysis is probably all nonsense. Self-congratulatory nonsense. How was yesterday?"

"Gimper refused to eat his crickets and berries. Not strange, I guess. He's been moody. I think he's angry at Sage. Lots of hissing. And I stepped in a puddle when I went to court. Sorry about that, ma'am. I scrubbed my shoes. Not a speck of mud inside, and—"

Pan clamped his mouth over a spoonful of porridge as Mistress's grin widened. It couldn't be helped. He had to cram a day's worth of talking into breakfast before the woman disappeared to the library and her inkwell.

"How did this last one lie to the court?" Mistress asked. "You never say."

"I don't know. I didn't ask."

"But he was guilty."

"Yes, ma'am. I guess so."

"You guess so? You've no curiosity?"

Sometimes, the way Mistress stared, Pan worried the woman was matching puzzle pieces and would realize her servant didn't always know what silent nods otherwise implied. That wasn't lying though. No, no, no. Lies were falsehoods, not silence.

"What if they did nothing wrong?" Pan asked.

"That's for the court to decide, not us."

"What if they lied for a good reason or because they had to?"

"And if you found out they'd lied to protect a murderer? Wouldn't that make your task easier?"

"I guess so. The groundkeeper said the next one's truly terrible."

He punctuated the sentence with a shrug.

"Bad form," Mistress corrected. Pan straightened. "There. Now, tell me what's going on in that head of yours that you're pretending to be so dull."

"Well, ma'am, in the place before here, there was a boy who collected eggs, and one time, he tripped and broke them. No one got their egg for breakfast, and if the other boys in the bunkhouse heard that, they'd have kicked him black and blue. So he said a hen knocked the basket over."

"I see. But this boy—some other boy—told you the truth, because he knew you wouldn't kick him, hmm?"

Pan plopped a dollop of porridge onto his tongue, all mush like any words he might have mustered, and Mistress tilted her head.

"Well," the woman said. "Not all lies are illegal. This boy didn't lie to the court or some other authority, and I imagine no harm came of it. Surely you remember the first time at court, when I went with you. The accused man had lied about killing a girl, and then nearly got another man executed for it."

"I don't remember that bit, ma'am. They said loneliness made him mad."

"Something made him mad. He murdered her, testified against an innocent man, and then seemed to believe his own lies. That's madness of a kind."

Sometimes, family or friends waited to comfort and take the punished home, assuming the offense had been no worse than perjury. No one had so much as waved at that man between the acid and hanging. That detail, Pan recalled perfectly.

Mistress ran fingers along the table edge as though turning one of pages where she found all of life's answers.

"Pan, you understand, don't you? That man lied at court, and it would have hurt someone innocent. Stopping that is justice."

"Because someone else would suffer."

"Indeed."

"Like that day you came to the bunkhouse, when Selli said my drawing of Sailseam Street was his. If you'd believed him, I'd be gone. I'd be in the quarry hauling rocks."

Or worse. Perhaps he'd be chiseling and polishing nosebleed rocks, which were famous for both their purple coloring and their effect on workers. Once the nosebleeds started, a worker moved on in a hurry or that was just the beginning.

Mistress chuckled.

"If you were in the quarry, how gorgeous your rock drawings would be. That you draw such realism from memory is astounding. I'm sure the quarry wouldn't give you honey for your porridge though. A crime, that."

Pan shifted, his feet scuffing across the floor.

"I guess quarry work isn't suffering," he said. "Not like getting the noose. Selli didn't tell a very bad lie."

"Oh, now. Hold the reins. Comparison's not my point."

"But the man who went mad almost got someone else killed. You said...I see, ma'am."

"Do you?"

"People who get acid told big lies—serious lies—that could kill other people."

"The court's not always on the verge of killing someone. That's..." Mistress's fingers tapped together, and she grumbled something about children and simplicity of explanation. "Don't lie to authority, and no one gets hurt. Let's put it that way. Justice, as the court words it, gives no preference to circumstance."

***

This vial had no name, and what an oddity that was. Mistress labeled each one with cloth and ink, the accused's name noted for all to see. If the accused were found innocent, the vial was emptied onto the courtyard's walkway so the public might watch acid hiss and bubble on a stone long since warped.

No name. Odd.

Pan turned the vial over and over in his hands, curious when pounding erupted in the courtroom. He saw nothing of the uproar from his bench, but guards at the doorway chattered.

"The black hound would drag her to the void himself!"

"They never found the body, so how do they know she lied?"

"That's right, you lump. No body. Only hands. She'd be hanging if there were more. She's lucky she's only a beggar and only caught in a lie."

"You believe that beggar rubbish? Look at her staring down her nose at everyone."

"No one knows who she is! She's a right banshee out of greytales."

Pan swung his legs, nail to granite, and leaned forward. He

remembered the groundkeeper's warning about a horror coming to court.

Maybe Mistress was right. Maybe some people deserved acid for serious lies, but liar acid was no less cruel, and little lies couldn't warrant such punishment. How lies were then measured, Pan didn't know. His thoughts swirled with the acid, certain of one truth: acid was for people lying upward. Upward lies—lies to authority—were the dangerous ones that could hurt other people.

"Boy. You there. Get back."

He hurried aside as the accused entered the corridor, and expected to see a monster. Instead, he gasped and clutched the vial of liar acid.

A grandmother! An ancient woman with white and gray hair bound away from a narrow face. Her wrists were nearly thin enough to slip through her shackles, and the tear troughs beneath her eyes were collecting just that. When her gaze caught Pan's, understanding clenched his heart. He knew that storming of fear and bewilderment—a search for anyone who might help, and how the desperation there might make a person do or say anything. This was why he never looked at their faces.

A clap of commotion carried the woman from sight, but not to the courtyard. Pan dallied, followed, and paused in the doorway. The woman was in a holding cell, a guard stationed outside the room while the others rushed about with unusual urgency. Such a change in routine, and each click of their heels growing distant tapped Pan's pulse.

What to do? Where to wait? He looked between the holding cell and the guard's back.

"Boy."

The grandmother's voice was faint.

"Boy, please. They've given me no water."

She moistened her lips, and Pan covered the vial with both hands, ashamed to be seen with it. She looked nothing like a monster, and so weak she might break from a strong wind.

"Are you dumb?" she asked. "Mute?"

"No, ma'am."

"Water. Please."

"I can't."

Her voice cracked. "Don't you know thirst?"

Pan hurried from the room, nearly colliding with the guard.

"She wants water, sir."

"I don't care what she wants. Go—" The guard bit off the word, eyes fixed on Pan's shaking hands. He marched Pan down the hallway with gruff words: "You can get water over there, if you're so daft-hearted. Be quick. We're only waiting on the captain."

Pan stared at the fountain. He hadn't intended to personally retrieve water. He looked to the guard, who scoffed.

"Don't you dare cry on me."

The man walked away, and Pan searched for a cup or vessel. He still hadn't found one when hands seized and spun him around. The guard had returned.

"Little pisser! Did you help her?"

Her? The grandmother?

"Boy, speak up."

"Water, sir. I was getting water."

"I have eyes. Were you trying to help her?"

Was retrieving water wrong? Was that punishable? Pan sealed his mouth and shook his head, saved by a calmer guard's intervention.

"Stop harassing the child. You can't seriously think he was distracting you so she could escape."

"But he—!"

"You left your post. Leave him."

Pan's feet hammered down the corridor, passing the room where the grandmother had been held. Guards dallied there, flourishing a piece of metal and squabbling over where the woman had hidden it.

"We searched her. We didn't find no lock pick."

"And her hair? Don't tell me it was bound up on its own!"

Pan shot from the building, lickety-split over cobblestones until he gained distance. He stood at the corner with eyes fixed on the courthouse, waiting for a guard to appear and call him back, but he was again beneath notice. He couldn't recall anyone ever escaping from the courthouse.

Mistress had a peculiar way of describing unexplained twists of fate: gods and weights. Nicero sometimes balanced the scales of judgment to his own satisfaction, like that time Petals had disappeared after Mistress declared killing the aged lizard the most merciful course. Petals had turned up weeks later, having gorged herself on the rats troubling their pantry, and earned herself two more years and the most elaborate of charcoal drawings for her cage. Maybe the court didn't always measure serious and little lies correctly, in which case, Nicero intervened as the higher authority.

That, Pan decided, seemed the right order of things.

He traversed backstreets to an empty house and lizards. For once, the silence was welcome. The workroom was undisturbed, and a smoldering lump of juniper was quickly stoked back to flame. The crackling twigs, he later blamed, prevented him from hearing the door open behind him.

"Boy."

He stared at Sage, thinking the lizard had finally spoken. He didn't know whether to be happy or terrified by that.

"Boy, please."

The grandmother stood at the door.

"No," Pan whispered, and louder: "You can't be here. Why are you here?"

"I have no family. No friends. No home. You're the only one who's shown me kindness, and they'll make a racket soon—have every leper and rat looking for me. Please. Hide me today, and Nicero will remember your good deed for eternity."

Silence afforded him no answer. She ignored his shaking head, even as his back pressed against the cages as though he might join the lizards in their safe observation of the world. If his existence were forever unnoticed, he might at least be sheltered.

"Boy, I'm not trying to frighten you. This smell..." The woman motioned at herself. "I was hiding among rubbish baskets in the alley. I'm not spry enough to outrun an entire guardhouse. I had nowhere to go and could draw no attention to myself, and then you passed, like the Journeyman's evening star, to give me hope. You know all the backstreets and how to go about unseen, don't you?"

"Ma'am, you really shouldn't be here."

"What is your name? Let me thank you by name."

"...Pan."

"A nice name." Her face softened, voice gentle. "I promise not to hurt you. One day, Pan?"

Without an answer, she inspected the storage closet, so near him he could count the buttons on her dress. It was a thud that broke him from immobility, and he bent to retrieve the item that had fallen from her pocket: a signet ring marked by a patterned shield and mountains capped in snow. It was surely a family crest, and an old one since such rings distinguished nobility.

"Is this real gold?" he asked.

The woman plucked the ring from his hands with a sneer.

"Mine. Don't touch what isn't yours."

"I'm sorry, ma'am."

"You'll forget you ever saw it."

Pan shrank back. The woman sighed and fluttered a hand.

"Apologies, Pan. I shall be there, behind those boxes. It is the nicest home I'll have known for some time, and even with no company, that's better than bad company. Or," she said with a half-laugh, "company that doesn't want you. I know you'll do the right thing. I sense the goodness in you."

She disappeared into the closet, swallowed by its darkness. For the rest of the day, Pan felt her constant attention to his every move.

***

Pan stood at the chalkboard, writing Mistress's orders in the early morning light. The woman fiddled with a window latch.

"Rust," Mistress said. "I guess it's been a few years. A decade? These haven't been cleaned since before your arrival. Add that to the list. Clean the latches."

Latches? L? The straight letter with a foot?

Pan stared at the woman's back, chalk frozen against slate.

"There must be something for rust," Mistress continued. "Maybe..."

Snap!

Pan hadn't the courage to look up. He stared at the floor as he spoke.

"The chalk fell somewhere, ma'am."

"Well, leave it. There's more in the closet."

Yes, the closet where *she* had gone. Pan stared at the half-open door and then a bowl of burning juniper. Someone had broken and added thick pieces of wood to the embers last night, and as far as he could tell, had done so without the pliers boxed on a nearby shelf. The grandmother must have done it, but she looked too frail.

"Pan. Pan?"

"Yes, ma'am?"

"I'm afraid that, scholar as I am, I have no expertise with rust."

"Maybe vinegar, ma'am. I can try that."

He studied the empty chalkboard with a knot in his stomach. He couldn't go back to the bunkhouse, and he couldn't go to the quarry. He must make the right decisions by Mistress and keep in her graces.

His gaze again jumped to the closet.

"Ma'am, I think lemon helps. They might be selling them this season when ships come in."

"Brilliant. I'll leave you to it. Ah, and here's some more parchment. I snagged it from the burn basket."

"Thank you, ma'am."

"I look forward to your next creation!"

But Pan knew there would be no drawing today. He hadn't the concentration for it as Mistress organized her satchel. Perhaps the grandmother had departed. Perhaps not. Pan latched the door behind Mistress and tiptoed toward the closet.

"There's no need to sneak," a voice called. "I know it's only you coming and going with that loose nail in your shoe."

The grandmother peeked from behind the boxes.

"Good morning, Pan. Are you well?"

"I'm alright, ma'am. You...you said you were leaving?"

She flexed her fingers and stood too close, but what could such an old, withered person do? She hunched to his eye level.

"Write me a letter, sweet young man. Take it to my friend so he might have a carriage waiting, and I will leave."

"Can't you write it, ma'am?"

"My hands ache. The bones, Pan. I can't hold a quill anymore."

She stared, and there was a prying to it like the lizards, unhurried but catching every detail down to the bob of his throat as he swallowed.

"No letter?" she asked. "That's alright. I thought that might be the case, and there's no shame in it."

"I'm not stupid," Pan murmured. "I have a good memory. I can write in my own way."

"Liar."

It wasn't a lie! He sputtered, words bouncing off teeth and gums.

"Hush now," she said. "Your falsehoods are safe with me."

A secret knowing creased into wrinkles when she smiled.

"Don't pout. I'm sure you pretended as needed to convince the mistress to take you in. A scholar like her could easily find a more educated servant, and letters are rather basic." Face red, Pan looked to the floor. "Oh, dear child, I didn't mean to embarrass you. We all do what we must to survive. If I had to do something horrible to keep my roof instead of living on the streets, I wouldn't think twice."

"You're a beggar." Didn't she already live on the streets? "Sorry, ma'am. That was rude."

"Oh, you are sweet. Look at me."

He did and marveled at how gentle her words were when her face was chiseled from stone.

"What good is honesty if you're homeless or dead?" she asked.

"If you're not honest and people find out, they get angry."

"That's why you're going to keep my secret. It's why we'll both keep quiet. Are you good at being quiet?"

"...Yes."

She glanced at a drawing he'd left out, considering it, and then smiled at him.

"Yes," she said. "I think you're very good at it. Quietly drawing and keeping to yourself. Listen to my promise now. I shall leave tonight, but I'll need your help with the backstreets. I need a route unseen to the north gate."

"That's easy, ma'am. No one walks along Washerwomen Canal at night. There's a bunkhouse there, near the gate, for orphan boys, but they'll be locked inside."

"Perfect. Tonight then."

But that wasn't good enough. He must run and fetch the guards, and he must do it now before they dragged him to court and accused him of plotting with this woman, however innocent or guilty she might be. He couldn't know these things as surely as Nicero. Perhaps he already counted as lying upward for not telling Mistress of the woman's presence. But then, he was misleading an elder as well now by betraying a grandmother's trust, wasn't he? Whether Mistress had higher authority as a scholar, or whether age held sway, he didn't know.

His stomach clenched, ever closer to vomiting. She'd promised to keep quiet, just like him, and that had always worked. Maybe she had also come from a bunkhouse. Maybe her tongue was stuck in trouble no matter how good she wanted to be. Maybe. Maybe. And she was so old!

But the court demanded words, and if she had lied to the court, it meant dangerous lies. That was the difference, he thought. That's why the groundkeeper had called her a horror. Perjury meant serious lies that could kill other people. If he told the truth, he wouldn't be hurt, and no one would suffer for her perjury either.

His heart pounded. He couldn't let the old woman know he was up to something.

"I'll be back, ma'am. I need to get lemons for the rust."

Which was true. He told himself this repeatedly. With the court a higher authority than Mistress and the grandmother, speaking up might wash away all of his little lies as well, even the silent ones, in case they counted.

He found and led guards to the house, so very anxious about having their undivided attention. That anxiety swelled as they stormed the closet with demands of surrender, but there was no reply. The closet was empty.

"She was here," Pan said. "I swear it. I do. She had a signet ring with mountains. I saw it!"

The guards searched the house, and Pan huddled in the work-room, listening to their boots plod this way and that overhead. Furniture scraped across the floor, but she wouldn't be upstairs. It dawned on him that there was only one place she might be so hidden, if still present: behind the cages and all those beautiful landscapes he'd drawn. If the lizards knew, they kept their silence, never lying nor helping. He'd learned the art of stillness from them after all.

"Sage?" he called. " Gimper? Lilac?"

He squatted to better see around them, and an eye of brown, not gold, peered between a crack.

The cages scattered aside, and the woman shoved Pan against the table, one hand on his throat, the other squeezing his nostrils shut.

"You'll never tell anyone my secrets," she said.

He gasped for air, and that was all the opening she needed to upend a vial of acid into his mouth. Bubble. Pop. Blistering pain drew darkness ever closer, a burn that consumed every thought, and for what, Pan wanted to scream. What secrets of hers did he have to tell? He'd done the right thing by telling the truth.

Tears stained his cheeks but couldn't douse the burn or scent of ruined flesh, and that's how the guards found him: a boy wailing and sucking water from a lizard's dish, his awareness spiraling ever deeper into an abyss. He pounded a guard's chest and willed the person to understand that he hadn't lied—that the grandmother had been in the house!—but the only sound to emerge was a whimper.

***

The crowd swelled. The street sighed. A hundred faces pressed closer to the fence as a woman knelt, her manacles scraping granite. First would come the burning, and as the harness pulled at her face, tugging her mouth wide, her eyes found a servant boy in his cloak and cap, only now the cloak had been re-hemmed and dangled an inch shorter than it once had.

Ilnia Winslen, the crowd murmured, the last of her bloodline, parading as a beggar to commit murder and dispose of the body, piece by piece.

A noblewoman in disguise, they cooed, never suspected by anyone until the guards had captured her at the family's countryside estate. How they'd identified her as the beggar sentenced on perjury charges, no one knew.

Pan stood at the edge of the walkway. No friends or family waited to hug the woman, and whatever wealth she'd gained from that ill-fated murder had barely kept meat on her bones. She would have died, he thought, even if the guards hadn't found her hunkered down in that vacant estate, talking to statues and beetles or whatever suited, but none of that mattered.

He felt more alone than ever surrounded by the public's jeers. The stench of their enthusiasm would take days to scrub clean, and as Ilnia stared at him instead of the crowd, her eyes sparked. If anyone, she thought of the ruined flesh behind his teeth.

The court's hand read her crimes. There was no mention of the lies she'd told a servant boy.

As she watched, Pan raised his hands and pretended to slip on a ring. Realization flashed vibrant across her face, another secret she could keep. Tied around the vial of liar acid was a perfectly drawn family crest of a patterned shield with mountains capped in snow.

The groundkeeper appeared at Pan's side.

"This one," the man said, clucking his tongue. "This one deserves it, don't you think?"

Pan didn't answer.

"Boy?"

Pan watched acid well up along the vial's lip, and made no sound or movement. Silence, after all, was golden.

Three Small Sacrifices

Janna Miller

Janna writes to keep ahead of her daydreams (by just a little bit) and has published a few. Otherwise, she is a librarian, mother, and minor trickster. Generally, if the toaster blows up, it is not her fault.

Once, when trees could talk and birds could rhyme, a witch lived alone, back behind the cypress trees where Spanish moss dipped its tendrils into dark, tannic water.Her house was built on planks and stilts and semisolid earth.

Visitors came by boat, looking for love potions, cures and curses. All easy enough, as they would dock on the front porch and call out in shaky voices, "Mother. I seek your help. I can pay..." And they would.

In the mornings, she would check her traps for crawdads and lines for catfish. She would start the pot boiling and the fire burning. The day was mostly about living, after all.

She was not surprised one daybreak to find a man waiting on her porch. He was large in every way and quiet and patient with dark, stolid eyes. He spoke, "Mother. Please help me."

"Perhaps I can, Son. What is it that you seek?"

"A life."

"A curse then, or poison?"

He paused, "No ma'am, I want a life brought back from death."

She laughed and disturbed nearby dragonflies into flight."Son, you don't want that. You can't afford this price. Go home and mourn and remember the good."

At this he stood and nearly blocked the light that had managed to filter through the trees. "I can pay."

The witch considered. "Fine. We can start...you may change your mind. You have a lock of hair?" The man nodded and pulled a soft tuft from his pocket.

"Three tasks then. The first is this: Find her voice."

The man looked confused with a flash of anger for an impossible task. "Listen," said the witch. The man stilled and closed his eyes. He heard waves lapping against wood, the chirp of a cicada, and the voice of a morning owl. He stepped into his boat, dipped an oar into thick water and was soon gone.

He returned a day later, knocking politely on her weathered door. The witch opened it and waved him to a chair in front of a fire. There were two pots boiling. One smelled of root vegetables and brine, while the other smelled of....morning dew and bread. Her.

The witch said softly, "We can sit and remember here. We do not need to do more." For a time they considered the steam rising on the second pot. Then the man pushed the bundle he carried into her hands.

With a sigh, the witch opened the cloth and shook its contents into the pot: a wooden flute, two smooth stones, and a limp marsh wren."Your payment now." The man stood uncertainly while the witch revealed a serrated knife.

"Your ear to give her sound." He hesitated briefly and then leaned over the pot. He sawed quickly, letting the extra blood mix with the water below. She gave him clean cloths and, later, ointment.

The next morning, she found him in front of the fire again. She checked on his wound and served him breakfast from the other pot. As he ate, he thought he heard a song he knew. "What is the second task?"

"Find her beauty," she replied.

Again he left in the boat.Two days later he returned just as the sun was leaving red streaks. She was on the front porch then, stringing some beans for later. She looked sad to see him.

"Good evening, Son."

He nodded politely, "Mother."

"Come in, if you like."

The man carried a drawstring bag into the house.He smelled and listened and then thrust the bag at the witch: a delicate white spider lily, pink marsh flowers, and a blue butterfly wing. "My payment?"

"An eye to see her shine."

She handed him a sharp spoon and once again, he leaned over the pot. She helped him to her cot when he was done, bleeding and sweating. She fed him soup when he could eat.As soon as he was able, he sat in the chair by the fire. With one eye he could see a shadowy smile.

"Mostly people want love potions and curses.They bring their sins and desires, I just give the recipe."

"I need the third task."

"You can still leave here and go home."

"She is my home. Please."

She paused before speaking, soft as morning fog, "Find her memory."

After he left, the witch bowed her head and wept.

After three days, he docked and heavily crossed her front porch, through the door, and to the fire. He carried a red leather-bound book filled with neat, looped writing. She pulled over the butcher block and laid the axe on top. Hoarsely, she said. "Your hand to give her body."

He nodded once, lifted the blade and then brought it down. After he fell, she tied the tourniquet. She left him where he lay and tried to control his fever and cauterize the wound. He raved in his sleep.

Some days later he could sit up and look into the pot. A shadow danced there that filled his heart.

He helped her pour the pot into the swamp after the moon rose then rested on bent knees. The light shimmered in water that never was completely still. A shadow gathered on the opposite shore and took shape. It danced across the bank and came to rest next to him, smelling of sugar and ink.

The witch gently sat at the other end of the porch with a shadow of her own. They watched the stars come out together. The man murmured, "This is enough."

"You will see her like this sometimes. Other times in the flowers you picked and the stones you found. She is not here, cannot be here. But your memory is flesh and can keep you company."

"Mother. Can you teach me?"

"If you wish to learn."

"What is the payment now?"

"You have paid, my Son."

They watched the world around them dance and bubble, while the air fell in heavy ribbons on waiting skin.

Cleaning House

Angela Boswell

Yeah, I'm sorry about what happened. You hear that, Maris? I'm sorry.

You know, "I'm sorry" can mean a lot of things. It can mean repentance, or commiseration, a request to repeat something, or just an agreement that things suck. I heard the last one enough times at Granny's funeral. Though, of course some people just said it like you say "trick or treat," like it's part of this ritual and there's no meaning behind it.

I never really knew Granny, not like you did. Well, she was Alice to you, of course. Or Allie or Al or whatever. She once asked me to call her Al. That was after she'd informed me she was going to call me Eddie. I was like, "No, I'm Lottie," but I was ten or something and didn't know Paul Simon from a hole in the wall.

Granny was weird. I guess I don't have to tell you that, but I've gotten the distinct impression that your definition of weird is in another universe than mine. I knew she'd gone weird after Grampa died back in the eighties and she took their retirement savings and migrated to Florida. Before that, to hear my mom and everyone else talk, she was June Cleaver. But afterward she was showing up to holiday dinners with tattoos and piercings, boyfriends and girlfriends. She even brought a very docile afghan hound one time and introduced it as her spirit animal. I'm sure you remember Queen Mab. I thought she was really pretty, but Mom said not to pet her.

Yes, I have concluded that you had a lot to do with her 180. You were basically Granny's--Alice's--manic-pixie-dream...something. Which I guess means you're sort of responsible for the storm-chasing incident that put a chunk of siding through her chest. I never saw it, but my mom used the phrase, "pinned to a wall like a bug in a display case," and that's all I needed to be scarred for life.

I'm not blaming you, though. I mean, if she hadn't met you, she probably would have dried up in the Florida sun and died at seventy-five, but as it is I was trying to figure out what she did to live to a hundred and three.

Man, it was weird going through her house. I volunteered to do it--nobody else in the family wanted to go near the place, but they gave me that list of heirlooms and antiques to find. It was like a treasure hunt, only I wasn't so interested in finding the family fast-cash as I was in trying to figure out this lady my mom had always tried to keep me away from.

Granny had books on practical special effects, nineteenth-century etiquette, the war on Christmas, the secret alien agenda hidden in the Norse Sagas. She was all over the place--there was even a book of inspirational Nascar stories. And the dinosaur erotica. I don't know where she got that, but I'm sending sidelong glances in your direction.

Again, not exactly stuff you don't know. It's just that everything I found only added more blanks to be filled in. And then there was you.

When you showed up at the door, I thought you were the land-lord. I was all ready to tell you I was working as fast as I could and we'd pay for the murals to be painted over--by the way, I never told you I found your signature on the ocean floor one and I thought you did really good work--but then I realized landlords usually don't come over at three in the afternoon with a bottle of wine. I didn't know what to say when you asked where Al was. But I suppose all my cardboard boxes tipped you off. I liked the way you asked if she'd "gone downstream," as though it were just a little thing, to die, just a continuation of something larger. And the way you didn't say you were sorry. Saying you're sorry when someone dies means it's not your wound. But you just put down the wine bottle and put your arms around me like it was our wound, like we both had missing flesh where Al used to be.

And we did. I hadn't cried at the funeral. The funeral was trick-or-treating. Nobody in Illinois knew Al. They treated her like those nasty little candies in the black and orange wrappers. You don't even trade those. But for me she was a Reese's to a kid with a peanut allergy. And to you she was clearly the whole plastic jack-o-lantern.

I don't know if it was something about you or just the effect of sharing a cry with a stranger, but it felt immediately like there was this bond between us. Though your suggestion that we drink to her memory couldn't have hurt, either. I don't doubt your claim about where that wine came from, because it was *smoooth*. Or maybe you brought brandy? I don't remember. Not that I remember a whole lot after the second glass, besides asking you if you were a man or a woman. I would never straight-up ask somebody that sober.

But your answer was great. Something about asking what breed of dog this cat was. You said you weren't purebred or a mutt, you were a tabby. I suppose you've had to answer that question a lot. Even so, sometimes I wish I was a tabby. Also, you said something about having lost too many people over the years. Like, you had no family left. I think I said something about how Granny must have felt that way when everyone decided they didn't like her anymore.

At any rate, we talked about life, the universe, and everything like we were the oldest of pals. I don't remember exactly what we talked about, but I remember it was just what I needed and totally amazing and when I woke up with my face on the table at one in the afternoon, I felt like I was the one who'd taken the piece of siding, right through my head. But it was worth it, Maris. Definitely worth it.

I don't know if I thanked you for helping me with Granny Al's stuff, though I probably expressed my undying gratitude at least once during our evening bacchanals. Probably around the time I told you I wanted to have your babies. I distinctly remember saying, "Tabby or no, I'm kicking science in the balls until it lets this happen!" Then you picked up that boxing nun thing and screamed, "For science!" and threw it at the Einstein bobble head.

Yeah, that was probably the best week of my life. Also the weirdest. And on the off-chance that I missed it while I was helping you dispose of Al's wet bar, I'd just like to say thank you. For making the job of sorting through my grandma's possessions go faster, certainly, but for more than that. Because whatever magic you wove over that widowed housewife, you wove it over me, too. And you opened my eyes to parts of existence I never suspected, though they seem to be slipping downstream fast.

That last night, when you took me to your house for dinner--well, I went in with one view of the world and came out with another. You poured me a cup of tea and started talking about mythology and creatures like yourself. At that point, of course, I still thought you were full of it.

The tea was really good, and this is coming from someone who usually hates tea, but it just gave me this feeling like everything was great. I was sure it had to be illegal, or at least it would be once the government found out about it. Still, as we were sitting there having our high tea, I felt like something was, I don't know, lurking. Like when you're home alone at night and you realize how much darkness is outside, and you close all the curtains to keep it out.

Well, maybe that's just me. I'd say that I've said too much, but we passed that point long ago. Like, if there's a guardrail that represents the border of intimacy, we sent a truck through that sucker. And if that didn't happen the first night we spent in Granny's house, it certainly went over the cliff when you proved to me that you weren't human.

Now, I'm not just talking about when you recounted your "previous lives" and showed me the artifacts you'd saved from each one. Or the fact that your house was a shoreline cave with several rooms that were underwater. I mean, that was pretty cool, but let's be honest, Maris--I'm talking about the biology lesson.

I know you've been familiar with more than one...species of people, I guess, for a long time, but I was pretty shocked when you showed me what the rest of your body looked like. Tabby cat, indeed!

After that, I was ready to look at anything and just shrug. Anything, that is, except the nets in your little tide pool garden.

I don't know why I stuck my hand in one, but dang--that "something lurking" business I'd had an inkling of before was nothing compared to this. It was like those windows I tried to cover had exploded and the darkness came crashing in and burrowed under my skin like so many tropical parasites. I could hear you laughing, but let me assure you it was not funny. At all.

Obviously I had never touched a soul before, and this was not the way to start. Everything these strangers in the net had ever thought or done, everything they'd rolled up into a little ball in their heart or whatever, just slammed into me like an Intimacy Express truck.

Of course, I was the one who was sticking my hands where they weren't supposed to be. Only after this lovely experience did you tell me about drowned souls in the water table and how they dissolve in the sea. Yeah, could have used a warning. I'm imagining a big sticker from the surgeon general.

But by that time I was so freaked out, I didn't even ask you why you were collecting souls in a net (mistake number one). All I wanted was to go back to Al's house and crawl into my sleeping bag in the middle of a cardboard box fort and stay there until morning.

But when I got to my box fort, I couldn't sleep. It was like the souls were anti-theft dye packets and they stained me all over. These jumbled memories buzzed in my skin like that time I washed my hands with paint thinner. (Wait, I think that might have been one of the memories. When did I wash my hands with paint thinner?)

It was easily the worst night of my life. There were some shell-shocked veterans in there, lots of murder victims, and at least one person who'd come out the other side of the Holocaust. It was like someone had taken history class and the evening news, put them in a juicer, and waterboarded me with it. I'll grant there were some good memories there too, but man, it was like trying to hear one person giggling while ten others are screaming. I just kept thinking, why, *why* would you be collecting this? I also thought I might be going insane. I'm pretty sure we drank absinthe at some point during the week, and that stuff's supposed to melt your brain.

But when it was light enough that I could come out of my cardboard cave, there was one thing I did know: whatever this was, I had to make it stop. Not letting these souls dissolve in the sea would be absolutely psychopathic cruelty. If there was one thing I had to do before I left Florida, it was to cut them free. Not only for their sakes, but for your sake, because I loved you and could not stand the thought of your being responsible for this. If I could release you from that guilt, then I would. You must understand, Maris, that I only had your interests in mind when I did it. How could I--or probably anybody--meet you, know you as I did, and not love you, not want only good for you?

So, I went to see you again. I'm sure I looked like a wreck. Your concern when you saw me only strengthened my resolve to do whatever I could, to do anything for you. I'm sure you've inspired this kind of devotion in plenty of others during the many lifetimes you told me about. But, no one else's devotion led them to the same place mine did.

You asked me how I was doing after all that had happened the night before (which was hardly anything, really--the things that "happened to me" were just things I'd suddenly remembered that had happened to other people). I think my answer was just a string of cuss words. Then I asked if you could maybe make me some more of that tea we'd had the day before, the one that gave me such a feeling of wellbeing. You agreed that sounded like a good idea, and disappeared into the cave. That's when I did it.

As soon as you were out of sight, the moment you'd gone around the corner and into the darkness to get the tea, I pulled out the knife I'd taken from Al's kitchen. And then I went to the little pool and put my hands out to touch the scariest, most horrible thing I'd ever encountered. But I did it. I touched that net of souls again for you — only for love of you.

It was pretty much the same as before. The way being stabbed in the face is pretty much the same as having your leg cut off. A distinct experience, but with an overarching unpleasantness that blots out any differences while it's happening.

It was difficult to focus on what I was doing after this onslaught, but I managed to cut the net free. And then the second, and the third.

By the time you returned to the mouth of the cave, I think I was lying on the ground. This had been worse than the night before, because I'd touched more souls. So many lives shaped by suffering flooded my nerves, so many images spilled across my mind. There was, again, some small joy in the tangled mess of experiences, but maybe those who drown do so as the capstone to a life more characterized by pain than those who die in other ways.

I know I already said it, but I'm sorry. I regret cutting the net and letting all the souls go. I didn't know. How could I have known? You hadn't told me. Maybe you should have, but then again *you* didn't know what I was going to do. I like to think you would have told me, eventually.

I don't know how long it took you to figure you what had happened, because I was really out of it, having flashbacks or whatever you call it when they're not your own memories. But yeah, when I was finally myself again, inside the cave where you'd dragged me onto that weird French fainting couch--when I saw your face, I knew something was wrong.

You weren't looking at me. I saw you standing there, with your hands together and your shoulders hunched. Now, that was totally out of line with your nature as I'd come to understand it, but the look on your face was the clincher. For a second I thought you were someone else.

I'm glad you didn't leave me in the dark and brood about it like some people would. No, you are a paragon of direct and to the point. Just turned around, saw I was awake, and said, "The souls were in the tea."

Now, that was not at all what I expected you to say. Maybe ask me if I was going to be okay or something, though I'm sure you're familiar with what touching souls does to people and you knew I wasn't in any danger. But it did take me a moment to figure out what you meant. Sometimes my wheels turn slowly.

I wanted to ask you how you strained out all the pain and terror, but thought better of it when I realized that not only had you been staying alive by drinking soul tea, but I had just dumped out your supply.

If it had been me, I would have thrown a fit. But I suppose you learn a certain amount of acceptance and zen-like chill when you live for that long. I remembered then what you'd told me the day we met, about having watched so many loved ones slip away, downstream.

Then it felt like I'd always known, like I just hadn't paid attention. But, I think I'm getting ahead of myself. You said that it took a long time to gather enough souls to make the tea--before that, I guess I just thought I'd basically ruined everything in your fridge but that you could go out to the store and replace it. But then you explained about how the souls coming down the river were getting more rare and I realized I hadn't just left your fridge open and unplugged overnight, I'd done this to the store of food in your zombie apocalypse bunker. The supermarket was picked over, and foraging wasn't going to turn up much.

It was sweet of you to try and console me that I hadn't done anything more than speed up the inevitable a few years, that you would've run low eventually. But killing anyone is just speeding up the inevitable, so really there's not much comfort in that. And then there was the little matter of the souls.

Part of me still wants to believe that what you did to them was worse than what I did to you, that being some other class of creature, you couldn't possibly understand human souls. But the part of me that wants to see you blameless, in the best light possible, believes you.

Because you said that they dissolved either way, only when you made the tea you saved out the happy parts of their memories. I suspect I'm always going to be of two minds about it, but I also think I'm probably going to think twice before so much as touching another body of water.

Then again, I wonder what sort of pain you've endured. You can't always have been the person I met in Al's house that summer. How many broken hearts, how many lonely hours of grief did you go through before you developed that strange ability to love someone like you loved my grandmother, knowing for certain that you would lose her?

I think I got a glimpse of how you felt, then. I mean, you know I love you, and I knew I was going to lose you. And I think that was the first time I ever really understood how love can be worth the pain. Maybe that means I led a shallow life before I met you, or maybe just a charmed one, devoid of loss.

Since I couldn't get a straight answer out of you about how long you had (though I did like your "well, I've never died before" line of reasoning) I asked if I could help you. If I could get some more souls for you or something. But no, you were all calm and poised when it came to your own demise. It kind of weirded me out and opened up this gulf, like you had all this unobtainable secret wisdom, and I didn't. But then you smiled, and it was like a bridge. A bridge made out of pearly white...never mind. You seemed near and familiar again. The person I knew.

I felt a little hurt when you told me to go on and finish with Al's stuff. I wanted to stay if you didn't have much time left. But then, when you agreed to come with me in the U-Haul back up to Illinois, I felt kind of bad, like I was wasting your limited days. Maybe you needed to be near the sea. I wondered what I'd do if you keeled over in the truck. Take you to a hospital? Watch you dissolve into sea foam and have to pay for ruining the uphol-stery? Bury your body in the woods like a serial killer?

But I figured I'd deal with that when it happened. Love is worth more than car upholstery, after all.

I thought I'd be all mopey as we cleared the house out, but you made me forget--mostly--what was going to happen. And, I loved the way you sold the landlord on the murals adding to the house's value.

Looking back, I think knowing the time was limited added something to our little road trip. Not that I would kill you for the sake of emotional intensity if I had it all to do over again, but you know what I mean. I never got the sense that you blamed me for it. You just kind of took it in stride, like, hey, that's life--or rather, that's death.

I did love the relatives' reactions to you, though — like they were confused because they liked you, but they didn't want to (though of course they liked the family heirloom fast-cash). I swear, you have some kind of magical effect on people. Maybe you get it from the tea, I don't know. Or maybe from the sea.

Of course, they're all inextricably linked, now aren't they? Souls go into the sea or whatever. The world just gets weirder and weirder the longer you look at it. And you've had quite the long view.

I could tell, though, that your view was starting to fade when we were driving back to Florida in my car. Something in your eyes, I guess. I thought about getting a motel room because Al's house was no longer available, and I didn't want to invite myself into your cave to watch you die. It just...seemed rude.

So, I was glad when you invited me. I tried not to show my relief, but you probably saw it anyway. It's difficult, you know, to spend time with someone who's dying. I'm sure you know better how to deal with it, be all suave or whatever. Play it down, and make the other person feel comfortable. You'd make a great hospice nurse. I know this, and I've never seen you with a dying person. It's enough to know how you treat a person who's having prema-ture grief.

It really helped when you talked about the souls as echoes and how a person could hold onto the echo of someone else. I don't know how you came to know so much about this stuff, maybe it's just a perk to being one of your kind. I mean, humans know a lot about calories and sugars. It only makes sense that a people who get their sustenance from…echoes or whatever, would know a thing or two about those.

For a while, our conversation made me forget what we were sitting there waiting for. Your ancient bourbon didn't hurt, either. I think you may have suspected my motives when I asked you about the actual process of making the tea, but honestly, at that point I was only asking out of curiosity and the knowledge, once I remembered our circumstances, that this was going to be something of a lost art after you were gone.

But, as you explained the process, the thought finally did occur to me. I tried, again, to hide what I was thinking. I listened carefully and stowed the information away for later. But, it wasn't that long. Sitting around the fire you built, burning some of the things you were never going to need again, I knew it was happening. I don't know how I knew, but that sort of thing was just what I had come to expect when I was around you.

I wanted to take you in my arms like someone in a movie, but that felt silly all of a sudden, too self-conscious. So I just put my hand over yours. I could see the firelight reflected in your eyes, but as I looked, another light was extinguished.

That was when I took you in my arms. Not for dramatic effect so much as to keep you from falling into the fire. For a long time, I just sat there and held you like some weirdo version of the Pieta. Then my leg fell asleep, and the fire was dying down, so I figured the moment was probably over.

I put some more of your broken furniture on the fire, though the part of your cave that was under the water would just have to content itself with natural decay to clean it. I never did find out what was down there, but a crappy flashlight I found among your earthly possessions seemed to indicate a foosball table and a refrigerator, though what use the latter could possibly be under water must remain yet another mystery of the universe.

When I had stoked the fire up again and collected your tea-making supplies, I got to work. I didn't know what would happen since you hadn't drowned, but I figured you were a creature of the sea, so your echo probably belonged in the water. I took you out to the tide pool and laid your body in the brackish water. Then I found the remains of the nets and dragged them through the water to see if I could catch anything.

The feeling came again, like when I'd first encountered the nets. Like someone was there--it was almost as though you had come back to life, and for a moment I stared at your eyes, expecting them to look at me. Then I realized what it must be, and I dragged the nets around the tide pool until something, some change in the feeling of a presence, told me that I'd caught it.

After that I stumbled through the procedure you'd described to me, boiling the inhabited water, adding the powders and straining it through the cloths. I don't know if I did it right. When I was done, I poured it into one of your teacups, but I didn't drink it. I just stared at it as it cooled.

I guess I'd been kind of in shock or something up until that point. But then my head began to clear and I bawled like a two-year-old in the supermarket whose mom said to put the Reese's back. When I'd finished my tantrum of grief, I looked again at the teacup, but drinking it suddenly seemed obscene. So I picked up one of the wine bottles we'd gone through, washed it out and poured the tea in there.

And that's where it is still. Sealed away on a shelf in my house in Illinois. I don't know how long I'll keep it there. I don't know if I'll ever drink it. Maybe I'll pour it in the sea. Or in a river that leads to the sea. That's where it all leads, after all. Even if you pour the water into the mid-continent dirt, the groundwater washes into lakes, streams, rain...sooner or later, it all goes downstream.

The Kingdom of the Butterflies

Isabel Cañas

Isabel Cañas a Mexican-American fantasy writer and graduate of the Clarion West Writers Workshop. A PhD candidate of late medieval Islamicate literature, she can often be found in the Persian poetry section of the university library, notebook in hand, daydreaming about Mongol queens and long-dead warlords. Isabel knows nine languages and has lived in Mexico, Scotland, Egypt, Turkey, and Jordan. She currently divides her time between Chicago and New York. To learn more about what Isabel is up to, including recent and forthcoming publications, see www.isabelcanas.com.

In the first golden weeks of autumn, when las monarcas descended into el Valle from the mortal world, Elvira finished her weaving as quickly as she could. She put down her shuttle and spent a moment stretching stiff limbs, relishing the heat of afternoon on her brown arms and light cotton dress after a long misty morning.

Then she stood, closed her eyes, and ran.

The path to the pine grove was carved in her muscles, in her heart. Never once did she open her eyes as she ran, trusting the sun-warmed earth and dry needles beneath her bare feet to guide her. Cooler air against her flushed cheeks and bare arms meant she was close; when pine fragrance bit the crisp air, she knew had reached the heart of the grove.

There she stopped.

She opened her eyes.

Butterflies covered the trunks of the pines, thick as serpent scales, their plumage ruddy as sunsets after a storm. The trunks quivered like the hides of living beasts, rippling and trembling with thousands of brilliant wings.

Every autumn, Elvira begged her older sister Rosa to come with her to see las monarcas. Rosa was the undisputed head of their little family of two, the one who taught Elvira to weave and kept her warm at night when clammy mists descended into el Valle. Elvira yearned to share the wonder of racing blind into pine grove with her. Perhaps it would soften the frown that so often creased Rosa's face. Perhaps then Elvira would feel that she was looking after Rosa as Rosa looked after her.

But Rosa refused. She remembered a time before el Valle, faces and stories that were strangers to Elvira. She remembered a legend of how las monarcas were the spirits of mortals who had passed on from the mortal world, who stopped in el Valle to rest in the middle of their long migration. When they left el Valle, they would soar over the volcanoes that ringed the valley and across la tierra negra beyond to paradise.

"They come. They leave. And we stay here." The finality in Rosa's voice was as brittle as dried pine needles.

So Elvira wandered the pine grove alone. She tilted her face up, drinking in the thousands of monarcas as they rose from the trees in waves. Their wings thickened the air, brushing Elvira's cheeks and arms soft as breathing as they soared past her, past the crowns of the pines into the azure sky.

***

The passing of time changed neither Elvira nor Rosa in el Valle. It was one of those gods-touched places that was neither here nor there, a narrow, soft-earthed valley with a stream flowing from the north and carving its way lazily south, past a cave where the girls slept, and a clearing where they wove. In the clearing grew twin young pines, their slim bodies bound by the ropes of backstrap looms. Between the pines sat a large obsidian bowl, gleaming with the seamless silky black of a blessing from the underworld.

Every morning the xolotl, a squat hairless spirit dog, shepherded a new flock of souls to the sisters and left them folded neatly as linens in the obsidian bowl. And every day the girls knelt before the pines, fastened the end of their looms around their waists and lower backs, and began their work: the weaving of these damned mortal souls into aguamiel, the ambrosia of the gods.

The weaving of souls was entrusted to only the most skilled and delicate of weavers, for souls would shatter beneath the heavy hands of gods. With deft fingers, Elvira and Rosa plucked feathersoft souls from the bowl and spun them, whispering spells taught to them by their master, the goddess Mayahuel, to silence their cries.

Sometimes the souls spun quietly, for they were tired and resigned to their fate as they stretched and transformed into golden thread. Others wept, crying out names or prayers to gods unknown to Elvira. When these souls passed through her hands, their sorrow warm against her calloused fingertips, Elvira silenced them as quickly as she could.

Once their spools were heavy with silk thread, golden as sunrises, the sisters wove. Only the rhythmic pass of the shuttle and steady breathing broke the silence of the clearing until Mayahuel arrived to collect the golden cloth of aguamiel.

Mayahuel was a quiet goddess, but that did not mean she was kind. She moved slow as honey as she entered the sisters' clearing, her rich yellow skin luminous as that of a golden idol. Her smiles for the sisters were cold, her painted teeth gleaming like a jaguar's after the kill. Her jet hair was crowned with a diadem of *maguey* agave thorns, her lips and teeth reddened with dye in the way of the women of Xochitlycacan, the city of the gods.

Mayahuel trusted no one but herself to carry the aguamiel to paradise. The sisters watched as she left el Valle by an unseen path, crossing la tierra negra. Once in Xochitlycacan, Mayahuel unfolded the cloth of woven souls and willed it with her magic to melt, to pour as amber liquid into the obsidian goblets of her brothers and sisters.

Under no circumstances were the girls to try to do so themselves, or even to try putting the aguamiel cloth in their mouths. Mayahuel warned them sternly that aguamiel was poison to mortals, and she would not mourn her slaves if they proved themselves stupid.

Rosa was convinced Mayahuel was lying to them. But then again, Rosa loathed her.

As it was with many things, Elvira knew this was because Rosa remembered a time before they were slaves of Mayahuel, endlessly weaving souls with their spider-like fingers. It didn't matter how many nights Rosa spent telling her stories of grandmothers and cousins and the smell of rice browning. Elvira could not remember.

Sometimes she tried to imagine what a grandmother looked like as Rosa tucked her beneath wool blankets in their cave at night. Did a grandmother have white hair like her and Rosa, spider-silk plaited into two long braids down her back? Was a grandmother like Rosa, delicate as spun sugar in the sunlight and hard as coal inside?

But then she would look through the mouth of the cave at the night sky, at the brilliant diamonds glittering in the raiment of

Tezcatlipoca, the god of night, and remember she was content with their existence in el Valle. Content to dream of butterflies.

Rosa was not.

One morning as they wove, Rosa broke the silence between them.

"You should listen to them."

Elvira froze. She glanced over her shoulder at Rosa's turned back. Her sister's hair gleamed bright as Popocatépetl's peak in the sunlight as she passed the shuttle back and forth, rhythmic as the burble of the stream. Had Elvira imagined her speaking?

"To the souls." Rosa did not turn her head as she spoke, nor did she cease her weaving. "They want to be heard."

The skin of Elvira's arms prickled. She glanced down. Every hair on her forearms stood on end.

She turned her back on Rosa, and lifted the shuttle to resume weaving.

Instead she paused, and stared at the thread winking in the sunlight. At the geometric pattern she had woven into the aguamiel. How many cries were bound into each golden knot?

How many people?

She clenched her jaw and thrust the shuttle through the next row. These souls were damned. Their purpose was to be turned into aguamiel, to be sustenance for the gods. She wouldn't listen to them.

That was what she told herself.

Deep in her bones, she knew she *couldn't* listen. Perhaps Rosa could, because Rosa remembered cumino and the names of aunts and stories about monarcas, but she couldn't. Even those brief moments the souls' cries brushed her fingertips before she spun them into gold were enough to make her heart race in fear.

But fear of what?

She pushed the thoughts from her head and wove hard.

Later, Mayahuel scolded her.

"Stupid child!" she snapped, shaking the cloth in one balled fist before Elvira's face. She threw it on the ground, and slapped Elvira's cheek. The force of her immortal strength snatched the breath from Elvira's lungs as she staggered to keep from falling. "You ruined it. Now fix it."

Rosa glared at Mayahuel's back, her black eyes flinty with loathing.

Though her face stung, burning from the goddess's hand and humiliation, Elvira hoped Rosa would not overreact—after all, the goddess was right. The rest of that day's weaving was tighter than the beginning of the cloth, and its edges curled in on themselves. Such imperfect cloth would not melt and pour when Mayahuel's magic willed it to. So she stayed in the clearing long after the goddess left for Xochitlycacan, unravelling the ruined cloth and beginning again.

***

Elvira's hopes were in vain.

The next day she finished her work earlier than Rosa, and raced blind to the pine grove. Though the trunks were bare of carpets of butterflies, she brushed her calloused fingertips over fragrant bark to remind herself they would be back soon.

A shriek shattered the the grove. Elvira froze, her heart in her throat.

Another shriek, but this one stretched longer, echoing through el Valle—until it broke with a sob. And another.

That was Rosa.

She sprinted through the pines, ignoring the branches whipping her arms and the stones cutting the soles of her feet.

Lungs burning, heart racing, she reached the clearing. Rosa knelt next to the obsidian bowl, cradling her hands in her lap, her cheeks slicked with tears. Mayahuel stood over her. Neither girl nor goddess acknowledged Elvira as she ran forward, then stopped short with a gasp.

Rosa's fingers bent in all the wrong places. They were broken, all of them.

Mayahuel whirled on Elvira, her face a mask of rage. She held up a small piece of gold—no, it was cloth. A small piece of aguamiel cloth about the size of Elvira's palm.

"There is no greater folly than stealing from the gods." Mayahuel's voice was soft, but soft in the way of the underbellies of snakes. Her dyed teeth glinted in the sun. "Consider it a boon I did not kill her."

The goddess tucked the piece of cloth in the waistband of her robes, and cooly ignored Rosa's sobs as she collected the rest of the aguamiel cloth. She straightened, an impassive expression settling on her strong-featured face, and swept past Elvira without so much as another glance.

A moment later she was gone.

Elvira stumbled forward and fell to her knees at Rosa's side. Her head spun with smell of salt, of tears and sweat and Rosa's sun-warmed hair. She kept her eyes on her sister's face, not daring to look at her ruined fingers.

"What happened?" she whispered.

Rosa lifted her chin. Her eyes were puffy and red.

They burned with hatred.

"I wove a piece for us." Her voice was thick from crying, but steady. Steady and cold and so determined that fear seeped into Elvira's bones.

"*Why?*"

"They get their immortality from it, I know they do." Rosa's breathing came in sharp gasps as she fought to keep from crying. "I know it. If we are damned to be here forever, then I think we should be as strong and powerful as them. I think—"

"But she could have killed you!" Elvira cried. Now she looked down at Rosa's hands, and felt bile claw at the back of her throat. "How could you be so selfish! What if she had killed us both?"

One look at Rosa's hard face was all Elvira needed to know that she had thought of this, and it had not swayed her.

Elvira pushed herself upright.

"You deserve this for being so selfish," she said. "Mayahuel is right. It's folly to steal from the gods when they have given us so much."

Rosa lifted her chin, looked Elvira in the eye, and said nothing.

Proud, *stupid* Rosa. Elvira was glad for the anger she felt, for how its heat smothered the fear in her gut.

She turned and stormed into the forest. When she returned, she came with fistfuls of strong sticks. She unraveled part of one of their wool blankets for thread, and bit the inside of her cheek as she bound Rosa's ruined hands.

Splayed-fingered as a frog, Rosa could not weave for weeks as her hands healed.

The xolotl clicked its tongue when it saw the damage. "Will you be able to keep up with Mayahuel's demands on your own?" it asked Elvira.

Elvira resisted the urge to look at Rosa for approval before responding to the squat spirit. She held her head high and took the first new soul from the obsidian bowl, ignoring its cries. "I've always been the better weaver." It was a lie. She willed her voice not to betray her as she silenced the soul with a spell. "I can manage."

The xolotl cackled, raspy and dry. "Ay, que orgullosa eres. Don't anger her again, girl."

"We won't," Elvira said. She felt Rosa's gaze on her face as she reached for the next soul, but kept her attention on the xolotl. "We've learned our lesson."

She wove from dawn to dusk to keep up with each daily delivery of souls. Rosa stayed in the cave, her back turned to the clearing as Mayahuel arrived, stony and silent, collected the aguamiel, and departed. She exchanged few words with Elvira, never sang or told stories, and stayed in the shadows of the cave as her hands healed.

Elvira should have resented her. And for the first few days of double the work, she did. She composed long arguments with Rosa in her head as the shuttle raced back and forth, as her legs went stiff from sitting with the loom tied around her waist and lower back. Arguments where she eloquently defended Mayahuel's actions as just punishment and silenced her sister's fiery temper at last.

But then, as she lay one night beneath their shared blankets, lulled to the brink of sleep by the crickets in the clearing, she felt Rosa's back shudder against hers. Heard her sister sniff once, then twice, before falling silent again.

She inched closer to her sister. One breath, then two, and their exhales slid one into the other, graceful as dancers as they led the girls into the land of dreams.

***

Rosa's hands healed imperfectly, but Elvira helped her relearn how to spin with crooked fingers. From that time on, Rosa spun all the souls into thread, and Elvira strapped the loom to her back to weave. Thus divided, their work went quickly. Perhaps Rosa was the superior weaver before angering Mayahuel, but now Elvira's long, steady fingers flew deft and confident across the cloth. She had always loathed silencing the souls, and though she never told Rosa, she was grateful to be free of the task of spinning.

Slowly, stories returned to Rosa. She laughed less, and never sang, but Elvira was hopeful that soon Rosa would return to her brash self. Soon her bright voice would soar above the pines, the monarcas would return, and all would once again be well in el Valle. As it had been, as it would always be.

Elvira's hopes were, once again, in vain.

She realized this when the xolotl appeared unannounced one afternoon in the clearing, panting.

"What did you do?" it wheezed. "What in the name of Quetzalcoatl's hideous feathers did you do?"

Elvira stumbled, then caught herself. Her arms were full of blankets, freshly washed and heavy with cold stream water. Mayahuel had come and gone for the day; the long warm afternoons were for chores and stretching her stiff back and legs. They had plenty of thread for the next day's weaving, so there was no reason why the xolotl should return. "What are you talking about?"

Rosa was too quiet, too steady, as she took the top blanket from the pile in Elvira's arms and spread it out on a sun-drenched stone to dry. Elvira's stomach soured, twisting with anxiety even before the xolotl spoke.

"I warned you not to anger her!" it barked. "Today she brought the cloth to Xochitlycacan. She melted it into the serving goblet as usual, but when she went to pour the aguamiel into the obsidian cup of Tezcatlipoca, it *screamed*."

Elvira's jaw dropped. Rosa took the last blanket from her arms, but the chill from the wet wool did not lift from her body, even in the afternoon sun.

"The aguamiel was screaming," the xolotl cried. "The halls of Xochitlycacan echoed with it—the screams and cries of mortals, and weeping. Children weeping!" It shook its head vigorously, as if to clear it from the memory.

The gooseflesh rippled up Elvira's arms. She turned to her sister.

Rosa's face was stony, her jaw set.

"You did that!" Elvira cried. "I know it was you. It must have been you. How did you do it?"

Rosa said nothing.

"I can't believe you." Elvira's heart raced now. "Why would you do that?"

She thought of how white Rosa's face went beneath her tan as Elvira bound each mangled finger between stiff twigs to heal. What punishment would Mayahuel dole out next? Trick a god once, and they may forget the insult, but trick them twice...

"They should know our suffering." Venom stung the air when Rosa spoke at last.

"They will know *your* suffering," the xolotl cried. "Mayahuel is on my heels. Gods help you, wretched girls."

It vanished into thin air with a sharp crack.

Elvira turned to Rosa, opened her mouth to speak...but it was already too late.

Mayahuel descended on el Valle like a storm cloud, thundering and heavy with unshed rage. Other gods followed followed in her wake. Dark Tezcatlipoca, god of night and sorcery, appeared at her right. His face was painted with thick stripes of ceremonial black, his diadem an obsidian mirror reflecting the shadows and smoke of the underworld. In his hand he carried an obsidian spear, the base of the blade adorned with a train of his brother Quetzalcoatl's long emerald feathers. At her left strode Xipe Totec, the burnished-skin god of gold, his skirt—made of flayed human skin—swaying with each step.

To the girls' left, glimmering Chalchiuhtlicue rose from the stream bed, her jade skirts dripping water. Her bottomless eyes fixed on the girls as she poured hungrily into the clearing.

Elvira grabbed Rosa's hand. Rosa gasped in pain; Elvira loosened her grip. She fought the urge to step back, to turn and flee as her thundering heart begged her to do. It was no use. There was no running, no hiding.

They were cornered.

Mayahuel pointed one long finger at Rosa as she glided across the clearing, devouring the space between her and the girls.

"You," she whispered.

Elvira's heart throbbed in her throat. She stared at Mayahuel, but all she could see were Rosa's shattered fingers, all she could hear was Rosa's lullabies, Rosa's laughter, filling el Valle with the same lilting waves as butterflies rising from the pines.

She whispered a silencing spell. And then she spoke.

"It was me." She jutted her chin forward, feigning Rosa's insolence, Rosa's hubris.

Every pair of eyes in the clearing, mortal and immortal, snapped to her.

Rosa opened her mouth to speak—but no words came out.

It was a guess, a shot in the dark, but Elvira was right: the spells to silence the dead worked on once-mortal weavers as well.

Mayahuel blinked in surprise, but recovered with the speed of a predator. "You," she repeated. "How dare you—"

"How dare I be a better weaver than you?" Was it fear or anger that loosened Elvira's tongue? She barely recognized the voice that rang through the clearing. She kept her eyes on the maguey thorns of Mayahuel's diadem, too cowardly to lower her gaze reddened teeth. "Did I embarrass you before your sisters and brothers? You boast that you are the inventor of weaving, but your hands are too heavy and clumsy to make aguamiel yourself. You know as well as I how difficult it is to silence the souls with magic, yet not only do I do it every day, I've now spun spells into the aguamiel to release their cries when I command them to. You're not angry because mortals humiliated you, you're angry because mortals bested you."

Mayahuel's lips paled beneath their dye, tightening in anger.

"Did we come here to listen to you be mocked by mortals or for blood?" Xipe Totec's human-flesh skirt swung as he shifted his weight impatiently.

"I tire of your games, Mayahuel." Tezcatlipoca's voice was the growl of a jaguar, velvet, dark, and deep as it rippled through Elvira's bones. She was suddenly aware of how clammy her palms were; how despite the pain, Rosa clutched her hand so tight her fingertips had begun to tingle.

"Decide on a punishment," Tezcatlipoca ordered his sister. "And let us be done with this."

Visions of Rosa weeping in the clearing, fingers shattered, flashed through Elvira's mind.

Mayahuel opened her mouth to reply, but Elvira spoke over her, words springing to her tongue before she could think them through.

"Why don't we see who is the better weaver, once and for all?" she said. Her lifted chin was a challenge, but the haughtiness of the gesture was hollow. Terror coiled her belly as her racing heart beat the time of each silent passing second.

Defying the gods meant nothing but trouble.

What had she done?

"A duel?" Chalchiuhtlicue burbled, curiosity blooming in her hungry eyes. The water dripping from her jade skirts had formed a pool around her feet, and she stood ankle deep in water.

"A duel," Elvira repeated quickly, keeping her eyes on Mayahuel's diadem. If there was one thing she learned from Rosa's stories about the gods, it was that the only things they loved more than obsidian and gold were duels and wagers. Aguamiel was ambrosia of the gods, but sport was their sustenance. "The winner will be she who weaves the most beautiful cloth. If Mayahuel wins, she can do whatever she wishes to me. But if I win, you must return us to our home in the mortal world."

Whatever that was, wherever that was. The thought of leaving the pine grove and las monarcas filled Elvira with dread so heavy and ancient she felt she could sink into the ground. El Valle was all she knew, all she could remember.

But Rosa could not stay here.

For Rosa, Elvira would to fight to leave.

So as Mayahuel's siblings began their own round of mockery of their younger sister, Elvira pried her hand from Rosa's and walked on trembling legs to her loom. She lowered herself to the ground as steadily as she could, and, summoning every ounce of courage in her gut, cast a haughty look over her shoulder at the gods.

"Do we have a bargain?"

Mayahuel narrowed her eyes. She glanced to her siblings and back to Elvira, then sauntered over to the second loom—left unused since Rosa's punishment.

"Bring me thread," she snapped at Rosa, not bothering to look her way as she lowered herself to her knees and fastened the loom to her waist. Rosa obeyed, meekly keeping her eyes on the earth as she handed Mayahuel the spool and a shuttle. She retreated, hovering near Elvira's loom.

"Brother, we will begin at your word," Mayahuel said, tossing her jet hair over her shoulder.

Elvira picked up the shuttle. Her pulse thundered in her ears.

"Then begin," Tezcatlipoca commanded.

For a moment that seemed to stretch into eternity, Elvira stared at the shuttle in her right hand. She didn't know how to weave beautiful images into aguamiel. She spent her says weaving common geometric shapes, never thinking of their beauty—for would they not be melted by Mayahuel and poured gleaming into goblets anyway?

A warm hand settled on her shoulder—a hand with crooked fingers. Elvira looked up. Rosa's dark eyes burned, and though she could not speak because of the spell, Elvira knew precisely what she wanted to say:

Listen.

Elvira inhaled deeply, took the spool of thread in her left hand, and began. Inch by inch, as the shuttle flew and thread fed into the cloth, she untangled the spells silencing the souls of the dead.

And she listened.

***

Hours later, Tezcatlipoca's voice broke the silence in the clearing. "The duel is finished."

Elvira jumped. So engrossed was she in her work she had not noticed how the sun slipped down to the mountains west of el Valle, how the shadows grew long and violet.

She rolled her stiff shoulders and stood. Uneasiness pooled in her stomach as she and Mayahuel removed the cloth from the looms, rolled them to conceal the patterns, and met in the center of the clearing before Tezcatlipoca, Xipe Totec, and Chalchiuhtlicue.

"Show us first, sister," Chalchiuhtlicue cooed. "For the mortal was the challenger. Show us!"

With a confident grin, Mayahuel threw her shoulders back and obliged her sister. Color burst forth as her cloth unrolled, filling the clearing with light. Mayahuel had used her godly arts to dye her woven depiction of the city of the gods heavenly hues: the bright pearl pyramids of Xochitlycacan soared above the emerald islands in the great lake, which gleamed jade as Chalchiuhtlicue's skirts. She had woven the gods' brilliant feathers, their glimmering ruby scales, their jaguar pelts, velvet as night past moonset. A portrait of Tezcatlipoca dominated the scene, his obsidian mirrors and topaz eyes gleaming in the deepening sunset.

Chalchiuhtlicue gasped; Xipe Totec nodded his head in approval. Tezcatlipoca, vain as any of them, tilted his head to one side. A smug smile twitched his painted face.

"And the mortal's cloth?" he wondered.

Mouth too dry to speak, Elvira nodded to Rosa, who walked to her side. They met eyes for only a moment. The sun was setting behind Rosa's head, crowning her pearly hair with an ethereal halo.

Elvira unrolled the cloth.

She did not have Mayahuel's magic, and there was no color in the cloth but the gold of aguamiel. But each soul taught Elvira their song as they passed through her deft fingers, guided her hands as she wove their memories into the cloth: their children, their grandmothers, their ranchos, their rebozos, their long plaits, black and gray and white. Elvira listened as the souls sang memories of their gardens, their birds of paradise and humble agave, and wove the smells of the cinnamon in their cafe de ollá and the cumino of their mothers' kitchens into the aguamiel. She wove the sounds of bags on backs, filled with a life's possessions, the determination of cracked feet, of worn soles, as they took one step and then another, paso a paso, across dry red earth to the north. A sharp note of grief cleaved twilight at the memory of the north: the final cry of so many souls, the sorrow of separation without hope of reunion.

They should hear our suffering, Rosa had said.

But the gods should hear their joy, too. So Elvira saved the smells of grandmothers' soft skin for the end, and with a row of tight knots, finished the piece.

The gods looked on in silence. Even the stream and the wind were still; not a drop of water spilled from Chalchiuhtlicue's weeping skirt.

Lips trembling, Elvira untied the spell that bound her sister's tongue.

"You remember?" Rosa's voice was barely above a whisper. Her dark eyes shone wet.

Elvira shook her head. "But I listened."

Then Rosa's face changed; she took the cloth and ripped it. Ripped it again into smaller pieces.

"Stop them!" Mayahuel shrieked, and casting her own cloth on the ground, leaped toward the girls.

Something soft pressed against Elvira's lips.

"Take it!" Rosa cried.

She opened her mouth, and bit. The softness dissolved on her tongue like sugar—

Elvira looked at Rosa just as her sister shoved a piece of the aguamiel into her own mouth with crooked fingers. Feral victory broke across her face as Mayahuel descended on her with Tezcatlipoca's spear—

***

Rosa was right about the aguamiel. Mayahuel had lied to the girls. Aguamiel was not poison to mortals at all, it gave them eternal life..

But Rosa was also wrong: though it gave life, aguamiel could not ensure the eternal perseverance of mortal bodies, especially not those met with a god's obsidian blade.

When the xolotl came to el Valle the next morning, it found the remains of Mayahuel's final punishment. Elvira and Rosa's immortal souls called to him from the clearing, soft and pleading as fingers of mist. The xolotl approached, curiously at first, hopeful—then its paws sank into damp earth, and its quivering nose tasted the iron soaking the soil.

There was no hope for their mortal bodies, that the xolotl knew for sure. But what of their immortal souls?

It sniffed the air. Far beyond el Valle, crispness crept into the air of the mortal world. And with autumn came las monarcas.

In a few minutes, the xolotl's work was done.

It sat back on its haunches and sighed as two butterflies rose from the clearing. It watched as they lifted into the sky and glided lazily towards the pines.

Silent Lullaby

Tolu Senok

Tolu Senok is an avid lover of fairy tales of all kinds. She enjoys weaving enchanting tales of her own, and always leaves herself (and sometimes others) spellbound in the process. Her true love, however, is middle grade fantasy, which she hopes to someday write on a regular basis.

Tolu has a BSc in Psychology from Kingston University and is currently applying for her Masters in Creative Writing. She lives in Dubai, UAE.

Now this is the tale of a peasant woman who went into the mountains to find a cure for her sick child. She carried the infant, swaddled in thin blankets and threadbare dresses, in a straw basket on her back, for she had no one else to care for him. With her she took a thick glass bottle shaped like a giant teardrop that hung on a string around her neck.

Its contents had always fascinated her; those pure white bits like broken eggshell suspended in liquid the color of fresh grass. Sometimes when she lay awake at night she would look for its soft glow in the darkness, and she took comfort in knowing its light was for her alone. But soon the bottle would belong to the one at the place she sought, for when she was a child she was told by her mother, "Should you ever wish to give your life for someone, give this potion instead, and both you and they will live to see another sunrise."

It was said that in a cave deep in the mountains lived a cruel snow witch who guarded a rare healing pool. Many had ventured on the path up the mountain range, never to return. The journey was considered so perilous that the wealthiest landowner in the village had promised a cart of gold coins and half of his own land and cattle to whoever could bring back so much as a drop of water from the fabled pool.

The day this challenge was announced, the woman had spent the last of her money on yet another doctor, only to be told, "Your child is incurable, and will die in three days." But upon hearing of the pool and the reward the woman had sold all she had and bought a sheepskin anorak, a pair of boots, and enough food and water for six days. She then set off at dawn.

Around noon the woman had reached the mountain trail. Before she went up she stopped to feed herself and her child. But the child could barely swallow, and she was only able to feed him a sip of gruel at a time.

"Please be strong my dear; I will heal you soon," said the woman as she heard his weak cries. Then she sang a soft lullaby to soothe him.

She thought she heard a noise somewhere. The woman stopped singing and listened closely. There it was again, a rustle in the bushes nearby.

A moment later out hopped a large hare. Its fur was darker than the deepest shadow. It looked up at her with eyes the color of a clear blue sky.

"What was that you were singing?" the hare asked, its voice low and rumbling like distant thunder.

"It is a song my mother taught me," the woman replied. "I sing it to my son whenever he is upset or in pain."

"Sing it again," the hare said.

So the woman sang again, and when she was done the hare closed its eyes and nodded.

"I can hear the sorrow in your voice," it said. "That is the song of the comforting mother, who calms her child in the face of despair. Fear not, for I have heard you. Whenever you cannot find your voice, sing the lullaby and I shall come to your aid." Then it turned into mist and disappeared.

The woman finished eating and started to make her way up the mountainside. The path was long and twisting and the wind blew piercing arrows into her skin, but she marched on, thinking only of her son's laughter and how she wished to hear it again.

Even as night fell she still walked, with only the moon to light her way. But as the hours passed the woman's steps became slower and heavier, until it felt like she was dragging the weight of the earth behind her. Still she clung to the potion round her neck and swore she would live to see another sunrise.

In the light of the dawn, another obstacle soon made itself known. After the woman had crawled up yet another steep slope she stood and found herself facing a wall of jagged rock and ice. She thought about trying to scale it, but was worried about falling and hurting herself or her child. The woman fell to her knees. How would she ever get past this? There was no other way up the mountain. Was it truly hopeless?

At that moment the child started crying again. The woman's heart ached. She did not wish for him to feel even the slightest bit of her own anxiety and doubt, but the more she tried to muster her courage for his sake, the more the wall loomed over her.

As the woman stared up at its impossible height, she was reminded of what her mother always told her as a child whenever she felt incapable of something or wanted to give up. Perhaps those words could give hope to both of them now.

So she turned her head and said to her son, "My dear, you have a spirit of fire. Your flame cannot be put out by tears or stormy weather. It burns from within and lights your way. It melts away all that stands between you and what you seek. Remember the gift of your undying heart."

The moment she said this, the ground began to tremble. Thinking it was the start of an avalanche the woman became frightened. Only one thing could help them escape death. She took hold of the potion and reached for the cork to open it.

It was the sound of cracking in front of her that made her stop and look up. Ice and stone broke off and fell as the wall opened its flaming blue eyes and gaping pitch-dark mouth.

"Dear woman, I have heard your words," boomed a voice from within the open mouth. "It is the speech of the inspiring mother, who encourages and uplifts her child so they may grow in their inner strength. Do not let your own strength falter, for you shall have safe passage if you trust those words as your child trusts you." Then the mouth grew until it stretched from top to bottom, revealing a tunnel that appeared to lead into nothingness.

The woman stood up. With a deep breath of icy cold air, she stepped inside. As she did so a small flame appeared before her. It flickered in the air as it went ahead of the woman, lighting the tunnel a few steps ahead. The woman followed and hoped she would reach her destination soon.

The woman did not know for how long she walked. In the tunnel there was no sunrise or sunset, but only the light of the flame in front of her. Time stretched on into eternity.

She stopped a few times to rest, eat, and feed her child, and the flame stayed with her. It was during one of those times that she took her son off her back and noticed his breathing was heavy. The woman placed a hand on his forehead, but had to draw it away such was the burning sensation from when she touched his skin. She placed her forehead on the frosty stone wall then pressed it against the child's forehead to cool it. When she was done she placed her son in the basket, pulled the woven straps over her shoulders, and stood. Then she walked again and did not stop.

After what felt like an age, the woman came across a glowing blue river. On the other side she could just about see the end of the tunnel. She set the child down and entered the river. The water went up to her shoulders. If she held her child above her head, then perhaps they could both make it across.

So step-by-step the woman made her way across the river. She trod carefully, for the rocks below were slippery and uneven, and a single hasty motion could drag them both underwater. When the woman lowered her foot halfway across the river, the ground beneath it crumbled and her foot became trapped in a tight hole.

As she pulled and tugged to no avail, the current grew stronger and the water began to rise. She panicked and struggled even harder, but then she looked up at her child and realized how easy it would be to lose her balance and drop him. So the woman chose to ease her foot out carefully, and stay standing for as long as she could.

A long time passed. The woman's foot was still stuck, her arms had grown numb and shaky and the water was now above her chin. There was no way to reach the potion without sinking her son into the fast river. All she could do was hold him up until the very end.

The woman thought of the last time she had been this close to drowning. She had been a child and run too close to the river's edge. She had fallen in and been swept downstream. When she woke up she found herself being carried by her dripping wet mother to safety. That night she'd asked her mother how they had survived, for she knew her mother could not swim either.

As the waters rushed over her head, the woman closed her eyes and recited the chant her mother had taught her back then.

"Whether you be a raging river,

Or the depths of a bottomless lake,

To your grave I shall not deliver,

My loved one you shall not take!"

At that moment the woman heard a tinkling sound, like the clear laughter of hundreds of tiny bells. She opened her eyes and discovered she had not drowned. A creature resembling a young girl with smooth, ghostly pale mottled skin was floating in front of her. She had hair like strands of silken ice and stared at her with huge silver eyes.

"My dear sister, I have heard your chant," she said. "It is the vow of the enduring mother, who stands by her child in all seasons and circumstances. Even the rising waters could not pull you down to the riverbed. For your perseverance, allow us to lift you up."

The tinkling sound rang in the woman's ears as many smaller creatures filled the water and swam around her ankle. They grabbed her boot with their webbed hands and pushed and pulled until they had dislodged it. The first creature lifted her hands and the woman and child were raised out of the river. Water flowed out of the woman's hair and clothes until they were bone dry. Then the two of them floated to the other side and out of the tunnel.

The woman landed on a snowy plateau in the dark of night. The mouth of the cave was a few steps away. She looked down at the child and saw that his face had grown paler than the moonlight shining down on him. He could not open his eyes he was so weak, and his body shuddered with every breath. Heart racing, the woman held the child close and rushed inside.

Her footsteps echoed endlessly. The cave was massive, like the belly of a stone giant. Luminous ice crystals covered the ceiling. The woman slowed to a stop as she approached the center of the cave. Before her was a pool of still, deep blue water that twinkled like the midnight sky.

As the woman took a step towards it, shrieking laughter shattered the silence. She whirled round and saw a tall, barefoot, skeletal figure wearing a ragged gray dress and a rotten, stinking bear pelt around her shoulders. Her long white hair was frozen around her head in a wild halo. Her pinpoint eyes were sunk deep into their sockets and her pointed teeth glinted as she leered at the woman.

"What delicious morsel has wandered into my cave?" said the Snow Witch in a voice like sharp knives scraping against each other.

The woman knelt before her. "My son has an incurable illness and is close to death. Please allow me to approach the healing pool so I may dip him in it but once," she said. "Look, I have brought this potion, which is worth more than my very life. Take it, so my child might be saved."

The Witch's eyes gleamed. "I shall most certainly take it...once my wolves have feasted on your pathetic child!"

A gust of wind swept the woman off the ground and pulled her towards the Witch. The Witch ripped the potion from the woman's neck and the child from her arms, and then commanded the winds to lift the woman high into the air.

"Keep her there until her last breath has been sucked away!" the Witch cried.

As the woman struggled to breathe, she looked down and saw a pair of large, slavering black wolves emerge from the shadows and slink towards the Witch. The Witch held out the child with both hands, ready to drop him to the ground.

The woman wanted to cry out, to yell at the Witch to stop. But how could she when the winds had already stolen most of her breath? As her vision started to fade, the black hare's words echoed in her mind: *Whenever you cannot find your voice, sing the lullaby and I shall come to your aid.* So as the last wisps of air left her, out of the woman's mouth rang a silent lullaby straight from the heart.

The hare soared through the air and caught the woman in its mouth, pulling her out of the furious winds. Once it had landed it placed her on the ground and grew to ten times its size.

"Get the potion while the Witch is distracted and throw it on her. I will protect your son," said the hare. It leapt over the Witch and the child on the ground and landed in front of the wolves. With a smack of its paw it sent one wolf tumbling into the other, but within moments they had gotten up again. They bared their teeth and threw themselves at the giant hare.

The Witch screeched and sent spears of ice flying. The woman scrambled towards the potion, which had dropped beside the Witch's bear pelt. But the moment she grasped it, the pelt shook with great violence and growled. The Witch spun round and kicked her with surprising force, sending her rolling across the cave until she stopped at the edge of the healing pool.

"I shall soak your child's bones in your blood," the Witch hissed as it floated towards the woman.

Her whole body trembling, the woman coughed and pulled herself up onto her hands and knees. The potion had fallen from her hand and was now an arm's length in front of her. She knew if she reached for it, the Witch would lunge.

She caught sight of her reflection in the healing pool. It was so close, but her death was closer. She could only hope the hare would save her son, but would she have to give her life after all?

Go into the deep..., the potion whispered.

Its voice brought back feelings from long ago, though the woman could not understand why. She looked at the Witch's soul-piercing eyes.

"Soak in the pool first," the woman said. "And drown in its magic!"

Then she swept the potion into the healing pool and dove in after it.

The woman refused to close her eyes for even a second. But the water below was dark as the pit, and she was already succumbing to its depths. For a moment she wondered if she would ever find the potion...and that was when she saw it glow again, brighter than it ever had, within her reach.

She stretched out a hand, but her fingertips slipped against the smooth glass. The Witch's icy fingers closed around her neck. The woman fought against the iron grip. She made one frantic, final grab.

The moment her fist closed around the cork, she pulled it up and twisted the bottle away with all her might.

All at once the potion rushed upwards and straight into the Witch's open mouth. Her eyes widened in terror. The green liquid flowed through every part of her body. The Witch let out a silent scream as it bubbled and burned beneath her skin. Finally, the potion entered the Witch's ancient soul and destroyed it from the inside.

The Witch's body cradled the woman in its arms and rose to the surface. It floated to where the child lay and set the woman down beside him.

"Pour the water over your son," the Witch's body said, in a voice so serene it made the woman feel like a little girl again, resting in her mother's arms. Even the maimed and bloody hare felt calm as it dropped a limp wolf on the ground and watched them.

The woman took the bottle, which was full of water from the healing pool and poured it over her still child's head. There was a moment of silence, and then the child coughed and opened his eyes. Color returned to his cheeks and his face no longer held a grimace of pain.

The woman took the child in her arms as tears fell from her eyes, but at that moment she heard a thud behind her. She turned and saw the Witch's body lying on the ground.

Fear gripped her heart. The woman hurried over to the body's side. Its hair now flowed over its shoulders and its eyes looked deep and tranquil, but its face was gaunt and had a deathly pallor.

"I know the Witch is gone," the woman said. "Tell me, who are you?"

"I am the snow healer who once protected this cave," the body replied in a soft voice.

"How did you end up in the potion?" the woman asked.

"The potion contained pieces of my soul and some of your mother's life essence."

"My mother?" asked the woman.

"Yes." The snow healer's breathing was slow and labored. "When I lived here I would allow anyone who survived the journey to dip themselves in the healing water. One day a young woman arrived at the cave with her sick baby, but while I was taking the child to the healing pool the Snow Witch attacked me and struck me down. As she delivered the finishing blow, the woman threw herself in front of us and was hit instead. With her final breath she blew some of her life essence onto the child. So potent was the love that flowed within it that it entered me as well and healed us both. With my strength returned, I was able to flee the Witch and take the child with me to the nearest village. That child was you, my dear..." Tears streamed down the healer's cheeks as the stunned woman listened. "I disguised myself as a human and raised you there. So moved was I by that woman's sacrifice that I dedicated myself to learning the way of the mother and devoted my whole heart to you. I taught you magical words of comfort, strength, and determination. I gave you the life essence I had absorbed that day, mixed with part of myself so I could be with you always. I made that potion so that in your own time of ultimate sacrifice I could make mine in your place, and allow you to continue living alongside the one you loved most. Giving up that life essence eventually caused my body to succumb to mortality. Those fragments are all that are left of me and the life essence is the only thing sustaining them. This body is very old and has not received sustenance in a long time. It will not take long for all the life essence to be consumed. Therefore, I must relinquish it once again, so your real mother may rest in peace..."

The woman took the snow healer's frail hand in hers and squeezed it tight. "You are both my real mothers. I will love you for all eternity."

"As will I," whispered the snow healer. "Even if I fade into nothing...my love...will remain..." Then she closed her eyes and breathed her last.

The woman bent over the empty body and bawled. She clutched the child to her heaving chest as her long, loud wails echoed throughout the cave. A hole opened in the woman's heart that nothing in this world would fill it ever again.

When her tears had run dry she picked up the bottle and refilled it with water from the healing pool. She went over to the hare and poured the water over its wounds. Once they had healed, the woman filled the bottle again and returned the cork. Then she climbed on the hare's back and they left in silence.

It took an hour for the hare to reach the woman's village. It set her down outside the open gates and said, "This is where I leave you. Remember, sing the lullaby whenever you cannot find your voice and again I shall come to your aid." Then it vanished into mist once more.

The woman stared down at the sleeping child in her arms. She knew there was nothing left here for them, at least until she claimed her reward. All she had was her child, the one she loved most. The one she would have given her life for. No matter her troubles, she knew he was all she needed.

So with a quiet heart the woman stood and watched the sunrise.

Not Fade Away

Shana Ross

Shana Ross is a writer, mother, occasional muse, sometime wallflower, middle aged ambivert with a BA and MBA from Yale University. Since resuming her writing career in 2018, she has appeared in over a dozen different publications and continues to emerge.

The witch lived in such a cute little cottage. Well, little by Greenwich standards, anyway. Four bedrooms felt quite extravagant when the witch first moved in after her divorce, but one was a library and one was a work room, and a woman of a certain age should absolutely have a well-appointed guestroom, and, well, it felt cozy now. Her cedar shingles were perfectly aged. Her landscaping threaded the very unlikely needle between flashy and prim. Great curb appeal. Nothing, from the outside, that screamed "master of dark arts" – regardless of whether you meant "witch" or "new money."

This was the right address. The young woman standing on the front porch was both confused and impressed. She was knocking at the door of a kind of home that you see in magazines. What kind of a witch was she about to encounter? She began to have doubts.

Still, she had put a lot of effort into tracking down a genuine practitioner of elemental sorcery. She needed this to be real. She knocked again, too soon after the first raps to be polite.

Gabby yanked open the door before the girl on her doorstep could ring the doorbell. The poor thing froze, finger outstretched, millimeters before reaching the button on the jamb. She gaped. Gabby sighed.

"So, what do you want?"

The girl composed herself, re-centered her body over her tiny but firmly planted feet. Gabby didn't need to check her aura to see the earnesty flowing through her veins. It flowed like a river. After a rainstorm. During the spring melt. Bubbling until it nearly boiled. Babbling just shy of a scream.

"Hello," she said, softly. "I need a potion."

"Ugh," said Gabby. "Come on in."

The witch, a little unbalanced herself at the unexpected intrusion, paused in the foyer before saying, "Well, let's sit you here... in the sitting room." She waved the young thing over to a sofa and told her to wait while she brought some refreshments. Gabby hightailed it to the kitchen.

Her laptop was open on the counter next to her mug. Natalie was still on the screen, curious about the interruption to their morning video schmooze. Best friends at the Academy, they liked to drink their coffee together, chattering on about anything and everything as they puttered around their respective kitchens to start the day.

"Client?" Natalie didn't look up from the crossword she was now peering into, pencil tapping on her lips.

"Yes. No appointment, obviously. What am I going to offer her?" Gabby grabbed the leftover coffee and put it on a tray, then started opening cabinets.

"Three wishes? A glimpse of the sublime that underwrites our earthly reality?"

Some of their colleagues had noted out loud more than once that Natalie was an acquired taste, but Gabby melted for her. Their magics meshed well. Eyes still on her puzzle, Natalie smirked and continued, "Shortbread doggies. Second shelf, cabinet next to the fridge. And a small bowl of blueberries."

With a nudge from her friend, Gabby felt her confidence pop its head confidently above the water. Most witches took over established practices. It was daunting but satisfying to be on her own. She was steadily building a book of business. She was good – maybe great – at the witching part. She just had to remember that. The rest would come. But she couldn't afford to turn away walk-ins. Not yet.

The witch fetched the cookies, conjured the blueberries, took a deep breath. "Right, then," she said, picking up the tray, "Thanks, love. Call you later?"

"I don't have anywhere to be," said Natalie. "Leave the thing running."

Gabby wrapped herself in a quick glamour and strode into her sitting room. Nothing much – just a little something to give her brown eyes a pop of gold, tame the hair she couldn't control by natural means. The girl was sitting like a greyhound on the edge of the sofa, trembling slightly, as if that were perhaps her resting state of existence, rather than traceable to a particular fear. Gabby wanted to just hug her, instantly, but knew better. Boundaries. Besides, it might settle the poor thing to have some-one else in control of this conversation.

"So." said Gabby, and waited for the girl to begin.

She didn't. She twisted her fingers until the blood went out of them.

Gabby put down the tray and poured the poor kid a cup of coffee. She tried again. "So," she said, holding out the mug.

The girl accepted, and looked into Gabby's eyes, searching for something, but still said nothing.

"What are you doing in my house?" Gabby asked.

"I need a potion," she said, voice taut as piano wire, without any of the quivering betrayal of her body.

"Ah," said Gabby, and sat back to take a better look at the young woman.

She was tiny, but her limbs looked freshly stretched, like a teenager fresh off a growth spurt who hasn't had time to fill in around the new length on her limbs. The combo gave the impression of a vulnerable child.

On second look, that wasn't the case at all. She wasn't nearly as young as she first seemed. Young, yes, but from the perspective of a crone in training, most young women seem like barely ripe fruit. When Gabby looked more carefully, this one seemed to have an iron core. A weighty center.

The young woman put her coffee onto the tray. "I've been searching for –" She stopped herself. "Never mind. I have it on good authority that you can sell me a potion. Chiku. I want to Eat Bitter."

Gabby maintained her composure, but quickly darkened the room a tick or two, wanting a little extra shadow to hide behind in case her face became too honest. "That's a very informed request."

"Can you do it, or not?"

"I can."

"What do you require in return?"

Gabby held her breath. They were both intoning their words, as if performing a ritual for an unseen audience, and the deep ringing language in their heavy velvet voices, low and low and somber...it send a shiver up her back, and when she felt the tickling in her neck, she shook her head and yelped.

"AH! Enough!" She popped the room back into its natural light, and slapped a hand to her forehead. "Look, it's not what you want. Who sent you here, anyway? Have you not read enough fairy tales?"

Gabby gave up the measured gravitas and grace she tried to hide behind every time a client came looking for a powerful witch. She justified it to Natalie on occasions when Natalie teased her about her "witch voice." Fake it till you make it. Natalie shrugged it off and just said it seemed like a lot of work. Well, it took a focus she couldn't keep up right now.

That potion.

Why did it have to be *that* potion?

Chiku, mainstay of many a local witch, the all purpose potion, they were taught. A blameless draught.

Gabby couldn't stand it. Almost all of her clients, at first, came seeking it. It was a mainstay, after all. The kind of magic women whisper about to each other, the kind people want enough to come looking for.

Most witches loved it because it was such a straightforward potion – you drank it, it gave you what you wanted most. And so everyone got what they deserved.

"I know what I want," said the girl.

"Do you?" Gabby's eyes shot into hers. "DO you?"

"I know what I want," she repeated, but her eyes fell to the floor.

Gabby threw her head and shoulders back in a full body pout, the kind one associates with moody teenagers and Paul Rudd. Rudd-ing. She was Rudding, and couldn't help it, refused to stop herself. Maybe it would cause the client to think less of her, to doubt her skills and rethink this insane potion idea. She tumbled herself into a slump, halfway off the couch. She peeked to see if her performance had any effect on the girl, but she couldn't see from where she'd landed her body. She picked herself up and rearranged herself properly back on the furniture, which would have been a very long and awkward scene if the girl had been watching instead of lost in her own head, a single tear welling then spilling over, leaving a wet trail down, down, down her cheek and off the cliff of her jaw.

"It doesn't give you what you ask for," Gabby said, leaning in and putting a hand on the girl's knee. "It gives you what you want most. Even if you do know what that is, most of us are better off without our raw desires."

They sat in silence.

The girl finally wiped her face, and met Gabby's eyes again. "I want the Chiku."

"It means hardship, you know that? It's a potion named after suffering! What's wrong with you? It's in the name! It's a warning!"

"Please."

"It can't be undone, this potion. There's no antidote, no saving you when things go all wrong." Gabby stood up and began to pace in her own small room, the walls closing in on her.

"I think your cause and effect is backwards," said the girl, softly, like a blade so sharp you don't feel a thing until you look at where it's been and see the blood it's drawn. "It's not something that causes suffering, it's something you take when the suffering has already found you."

Gabby felt her heart snag on a sentiment she didn't actually understand. She wanted to keep arguing until the girl folded. Instead, she relented, albeit ungracefully.

"You can only take the draught once. The second time Chiku touches your lips, you die."

"It's a one-way ticket, no backsies. Got it." The girl smiled. Triumph agreed with her. She opened the purse she was clutching on her lap. "How much?"

Gabby was filled with hope. She named a price that she hoped would be a deterrent.

Alas, the girl wrote a check, smiling.

"Fine." Gabby took it from her, held it to the light on principle, pretending to look for watermarks or something. She didn't really care if it cashed. "Fine. But I warned you."

She left the girl and went to her workroom to decant a bit of potion into one of the cute apothecary bottles she'd just gotten at the white elephant sale, raising money for the local animal shelter. They were quite charming, and the aesthetics almost improved her mood. The last time she did this, she'd had to use a leftover takeout Tupperware.

"Don't. I'm begging you," she said, holding the bottle out to the girl. "You'll regret this."

The girl reached out. She took the bottle and cradled it.

"Well, house rules, I'm not going to watch you do this. Get out. Take it anywhere else, just not here."

The girl smiled, more beautiful than when she'd walked in, now that she was free of the tension that had bound her so tightly. Her weight was lifted. "I won't blame you, no matter what happens," she said. "I'm very grateful."

Gabby sighed and showed her the door.

"Chiku, eh?" Natalie was still fussing with her crossword when Gabby brought the tray of coffee and nibbles back into the kitchen.

"It's depressing. Like Women's Studies Sociology PhD Thesis depressing," Gabby muttered as she plopped herself onto the counter stool in front of the laptop. Her hands etched a figure in the air and her mug, freshly filled with hot coffee was suddenly in them.

Natalie shrugged. "You think she's a vanisher? My last Chiku client was kind of sweet. Wanted her cat to live forever. I mean, that's going to get ugly, but…"

Gabby's eyes flashed. "She's a vanisher. I'm sure of it. I've had six since March. The first one said she wanted to be free from other peoples' expectations. She went through a full box of tissues while we were talking. She didn't want to let down her kids, or her husband, or her sick mom, or not be there for book club, or forget to send her friends real cards and not just some online note on their birthday, or buy snacks instead of making them when it's her week to be class mom, or skip her spin class to read a book. I get it. I get it. But what did she want in her heart of hearts? To simply not have to deal with any of it. She took two swigs, sighed, and vanished."

Natalie clucked in sympathy, but shrugged.

Gabby started to flush, her voice escalating towards a rather un-witchy yell. "The next one was in distress at the state of the universe. She *said* she wanted to make a difference. But...poof. Then came the woman with a lover and a husband who said she wanted to stop feeling torn apart in her soul. So overdramatic. And so *gone*. The one after that said she wanted strength to deal with her grief, and the one after that, I swear she told me she wanted to fit into her skinny jeans for the rest of eternity. That seemed shallow enough to be true."

Her voice returned to a frizzled whisper. "The last one said she wanted to be seen, really seen, have everyone else know her true worth. Which, apparently, she priced at zero."

"Six in a row, Nat," said Gabby. "What is it with women these days, convinced to their core that what they want is to be invisible. To not *be*. I can't watch another woman fade from existence."

"I had two last month," said Natalie, putting her paper down, and for once, meeting Gabby's eyes through the screen. Gabby could feel an astral hug coming through the ether, squeezing her shoulders. It wasn't the fierce enveloping she wanted from Nat in person, but it was better than nothing.

"It just sucks," grumped Gabby.

"It's sobering," agreed Natalie.

"As a feminist, it's bullshit. It's – "

Gabby's thought evaporated. She goggled, agape, at something through the window.

She found her voice. "Nat, I need you. Here. Now."

Natalie sighed and winked out of existence on the screen, materializing on the other side of the counter. She rubbed her jaw. "Ugh. Makes my fillings hurt. Every time."

Gabby said nothing, just pointed.

"Oh," said Natalie. "Oh my. Well, *that's* not what you were expecting."

Parked on the street in front of Gabby's house was a little silver Jetta, and in that Jetta was a full-sized – meaning *gigantic* – bear.

Gabby grabbed onto Natalie's arm. "What do we do with that???"

Neither one of them had any good ideas. They argued halfheartedly for a bit, laughing before long, decided they were a bit peckish and shouldn't be dealing with bears on empty stomachs. They walked down the street to a cute little French place for pastries. When they got back, the bear was still in the car, the upholstery more than a little worse for the wear. The two witches stood in the yard, staring.

"What. On. Earth?" Natalie wondered aloud, with more tenderness than Gabby expected from her unflappable friend.

"I have to let her out," said Gabby. "It's time."

Natalie wanted to use a spell from a safe distance, but Gabby was determined to do this up close and personal. It felt respectful. It felt visceral. It would help her sleep better at night, she was sure.

Gabby walked up to the little car, Natalie at the ready with a charm that would stop even a barreling bear in its tracks, something that was usually a figure of speech and not quite so literal a concern. Nat raised her paper mug of coffee in a salute to let Gabby know she was ready, offering her own unspoken blessings to the thing in the car. She raised an eyebrow at Gabby, who crinkled her nose back.

Gabby stood for a moment, looking through the window. The bear turned, slowly maneuvering its body so that it could stare back at the witch through the driver's window, a small crumb of seat foam still on its snout, a thread of drool tracking back to its shoulder. Gabby put out her hand to touch the glass, and shivered when the bear put her huge paw of dinner plate and knives up to the other side.

She felt like this was about to be a cinematic moment of life, the kind where the string orchestra swells as two beings share a connection with the deepest gravitas before going their separate ways...but instead, as she reached to open the car door, she was hit with the full realization that she was releasing a giant damned bear from a tin can and had no idea what it wanted to do next. She yanked open the door with a squeal and ran, flapping, into her yard, little yelps falling out of her with each step.

According to Natalie, the bear seemed to think that was amusing, lumbering its body out of the small car and then pausing to watch the retreating witch. Nat certainly thought it was hysterical, and had the video from her phone to prove it.

But the two witches put their arms around each other for comfort and solidarity, even as they each tied themselves up in their own messy feelings about this crazy damn world with such people in it.

"Why a bear, do you think?" whispered Natalie.

"Dunno," said Gabby. "What do you think comes next?"

"Rampage," said Natalie. "Definitely rampage."

The bear huffed a little. She began to amble, then run, down the street until the road took a turn, and in a moment she was out of sight.

"I hope bear means freedom," said Gabby, "Whatever that means. To her."

"But, I mean, it's going to be a rampage," said Natalie, with a grin. "Come on, I'll help you brew more Bitter. There'll be more clients, come looking."

Gabby sighed, and made a mental note to set up a google alert for bear stories in the local news. Natalie was right; she would need extra inventory soon. Besides, it was nice to have the company, and the potion did make the whole house smell like peonies for days. The two witches went inside, linked at their elbows, to spend the rest of the morning bubbling and toiling, together.

The Remains of Prophecy

Rebecca Bennett

Rebecca writes speculative fiction with small town flair. She's based in Canada's capital and spends her free time as a friendly neighbourhood Associate Editor at Apparition Lit. Her short stories and poetry have been published in Strange Horizons, Bourbon Penn, Devilfish Review and other literary locales. You can follow her occasional tweets at @_rebeccab

"There's a crack in the ceiling."

Above us, the crack ran like a thin scar over the length of our bed. The night sky shone through the break, wider than it had been the night before.

"It's a bad omen." Hector's cold toes nudged mine. "If it's a spider-crack then it means death is in the house."

My hand settled over my belly, thinking of the parsley tea we'd bought the day before. "You already know there's going to be death in the house. Get back to bed; you need to haul hay tomorrow."

He ignored me. "It seems more lightning shaped. Lightning is good."

I pulled the sheets over my head. "It's just a crack."

"Gracie!" he hissed, smacking the sheets to grab my attention again. "Gracie! There's a shooting star."

***

I heard the news long before Hector returned home. The town crier shouted himself hoarse that the Queen had died in childbirth during the night, as a star streaked across the sky. The new princess was the Queen's seventh child. The King himself was a seventh son, with a pedigree and dynasty of his own. There was prophecy to the star's fall and the King announced that he would promise his daughter to a newly-born seventh son of a seventh son.

When he returned home early for dinner, still reeking of sweat and hay, Hector stared at our two children at the table and the four equal mounds of rocks outside. Emma and Charles scarcely survived their births. The others clung to life, blue and twisted, for only a few hours. Hector never spoke directly, never ticked each name off his fingers, but the words of the town crier – still shouting into the night – spoke enough for us.

Hector was a seventh son. With a lineage of his own: a dynasty of poor farmers with large families. There was nothing of royalty in Hector; you could see the workers' bloodlines in the breadth of his shoulders and the snub of his nose. The only promise he held was the luck associated with such a birth.

"The gods are good, Gracie." Hector's watery eyes were bright, the piles of gold he imagined shining through. He didn't need to say the rest. Birthing a seventh son only meant ensuring that that the seventh child was male. All we needed was one more, another son, and I was already pregnant. "First a falling star, now the lightning shape in our ceiling."

"I thought you said it looked like a spider?" Indeed thin fissures splayed off the crack in all directions, like a spider uncoiling itself above our bed. "It means death and you know why."

"No," he said earnestly, his hand reaching out for mine. It hung empty in the air before he knocked three times on our table. "It means luck."

His mother hadn't survived her pregnancy with him. No, Hector came into the world under the guiding knife of Mirwalda, our town's witch. Though it softened over the years, there was a raised scar on the side of his cheek from the graze of the witch's blade as she cut him away from his mother. My abdomen stung with phantom pain as I imagined the knife hovering over my own belly – I scarcely avoided the knife during the last two pregnancies.

I found no joy in childbirth; the pain always grew worse with each swell of new life. Of the two children that survived, Emma was my favorite. When she was born, she looked nothing like Hector; carrying my dark hair and watchful eyes. Charles was harder to bear; the last month I ached and cried. For the full nine months there was constant, painful, yellowish bile. His birthing took days, and when he emerged, Charles looked just like his father.

"You promised me." I pulled the parsley tea from its hiding place, a small pocket in my apron. The small cloth bag held just three spoonfuls of tea. It had cost us two sows to pay the midwife for it – a fortune considering the poor crops this year.

"This will be the last one, I promise." Hector gripped my hands with desperation. The touch was brief and warm, like all his touches were intended to be. His hands burned from the mid-day sun, grease and dirt still embedded in lines of his knuckles.

"I can't, you know that I can't." My stomach cramped at the

memory of my last pregnancy. It took weeks before I could sit upright without nausea or dizziness.

"This will be different. It will be our seventh. You know what that means, what it could mean for us. No more cold winters, no more hungry nights."

"There is no prophecy, Hector," I snapped. "There are just the lies the court tells the King." There was a small burn of satisfaction as his face fell and his hands pulled away. I should have taken the tea days ago. He had wanted to wait for the crescent moon, claiming it would lead to a speedy recovery. "What's the point? The child will die, just like the others. I don't want any more piles of rocks."

"You're stronger now; you could bring the child to term this time." Even he didn't look convinced by his argument.

There was still a part of me that wanted to believe him, that it would live and I would love it as I loved Emma. Perhaps I could bring the child to term, but I knew, just as I could feel the phantom knife over my abdomen, that death followed this child.

Another tactic then. "Think of the lost work, the lost wages. I won't be able to stack hay or clean the stalls. I'll be useless. With the late thaw and all the rain, we'll barely survive the year as it is."

"Think of the wealth, Gracie. The riches. Our bed is made of pine; the moon was waxing when we conceived. These are all good signs." Hector gripped my hand firmly, his breath strangely sour as he leaned in to kiss my flattened lips. "Next week we'll go to the midwife, make sure it's a boy. And then you'll rest. We'll hire a farmhand and you'll do nothing but get fat and healthy. It'll be worth it—you'll see."

He pocketed the herbs and shuffled me to bed, promising nothing but soft foods and quiet for the next eight months.

***

I did not believe Hector's superstitions. To him, everything was a sign or a warning. He left bowls of milk on our doorstep for the fey, carved runes into the corners of our house for protection. He wanted a reason, a meaning, behind every action.

There *was* magic in this world, even I could not deny that. But I couldn't believe it lay in herbs and tchotchkes for a man like Hector to wield. Magic belonged to women, to the witches that lived outside of town.

The child burned in my belly. A wooden totem that Hector bought swayed in a non-existent breeze, catching my attention throughout the days. It twirled under my watch until I felt the child spin in response. Every morning Hector prayed, blessing both me and the totem, as though my life was linked to the wooden doll. The toy would be an easy thing to burn or crush, but to destroy the totem would show I believed the prophecy. Besides, Hector would just buy another, spending money meant for repairing the crack in our roof.

I wanted a solution of my own.

Every forest path led to the witch's cabin, along them the canopy of trees turned into shrubs, and the ground became more muck than dirt. Mirwalda's home was half tilted into the marsh-land, nestled in the soft moss and magic that kept the building somewhat above-water.

Inside, Mirwalda sat at the only table in the house and puffed on a pipe. The smoke swirled and floated into the air until it was lost in the rats-nest of curls that piled on the witch's head. Mirwalda's eyes were bright and ageless but her body hunched, ill fit and sagging—like she was wearing borrowed skin.

The moment the door closed behind me, I told her the truth. "I can't have this child and my husband can't know."

Mirwalda laughed deeply at my words, her blackened teeth clenching the pipe so it didn't fall. "That's the first time I've heard that today. Probably the last time I'll hear it all year."

The witch tapped her pipe against the table. Letting the ashes pile at the center. The ashes blended into the other smudged streaks across the grain and the crumbs piled like molehills across the table. "Place your thumb in the ash. Draw a line and circles -- no less than two, no more than five."

The flakes powdered beneath the weight of my thumb.

"Good…good. If what you say is true, and you do not want this child, why didn't you go to a midwife? They have herbs: pennyroyal, parsley tea. Stonesee root grows like a weed outside of town. You'd get this for free."

"No, I need something stronger than herbs. A few days ago my husband hung a fertility idol he bought from a traveler." I hesitated under the witch's mocking smile. "I can *feel* it working. Please, he needs to think it's a sign of the gods so he can let go of this foolishness and leave me in peace."

Mirwalda tapped her pipe against the table again, squinting into the barrel to make sure it was empty. "A traveler? Hmm, that'd be Rhys. He's talented. Even the cheapest talisman of his is sure to work. You need strong magic to counteract that—won't be cheap."

"I have money."

"I have no use for money, you see a crown?" The old woman's knobby fingers began to stuff tobacco into her pipe. "I need a mule, a chicken, a new pot."

My husband would notice a missing animal. But the small pile of gold hidden under the bed, the coins that now clinked in my boots, those were mine. It was the only thing that was mine. "I can't—"

My fingers twisted on the handle of my basket. A blue gingham fabric covered my small offering of eggs and baked bread. Eggs were an easy thing to overlook at home, just a few skipped meals. A missing chicken would be harder to explain

Mirwalda chuckled lowly. "I know that look—you're afraid of what your husband will say. All husbands are fools. I know your Hector. Knew everything about him once his blood landed on my blade." Her hands rummaged over her clothing until she pulled out a small blade. "He wasn't born cruel—few children are—I usually make sure that only the good survive." She sniffed her knife as though Hector's blood still lingered on the blade. "He'd see magic in a pile of manure though."

"He thinks that there's a prophecy for this child."

Mirwalda shrugged. "There's a prophecy for all children. A promise in each whether realized or not. Life must have bittered you to forget such things."

"I'm not—"

"I know how to manage those seeded with bitterness." The witch took another drag on her pipe. "Magic costs, so does my goodwill, but my advice is free. What if I told you it *was* a boy you carried, would that change your mind? I'd bet if you brought that news to your husband, he'd find an appropriate gift in exchange."

For a brief moment I imagined it, let myself see the child grow into a strong boy. I could see myself walking home with the good news, prepared to spend months resting in bed. But each fantasy ended at the door of my house, ended with the piles of rocks that greeted me every time I returned home. "It's not about whether it's a boy or not. I know this child will bring death. It will kill me, I'm sure it will."

Mirwalda shrugged. "Anything can kill you. Still, you're the furthest along. Other women are asking for conception miracles. The miller's wife is further along but she's carrying a girl, poor woman left sobbing when I told her."

Desperation welled up; I couldn't return home to the mocking fertility idol. Hector only saw the potential promise of future riches, all I could see was the pain and illness that would linger in the meantime. "Please, there must be something you could do, something I could give you. In the summer I can give you some of our crops."

Mirwalda stretched her fingers, staining them with ash and drew sigils across her table. She hummed tunelessly until her fingers stilled. "Your husband, he is a true seventh son. His mother came to me once when she was young, always a brave little thing. Brave even when I was cutting her open." She wiped her fingers on her dress. "Many other villagers are counting miscarriages and bastards, but you have an honest claim."

"Please. I can't face more graves at my door."

Mirwalda held up a still grey-stained hand. "In my mother's time, long before birds had wings and stones were silenced, there was a saying: a seventh dynasty ended, a seventh dynasty begun."

I knew these words. It was a rhyme I heard often in my youth. "Woe to the mother of a seventh son."

She nodded. "Your mother taught you well."

"My father." Before he died, my father ran an alehouse. Drunks loved stories and my father learned the best. He'd stand behind the bar, shouting old fables over the din of the patrons. Most ignored him, but there'd always been an extra coin or two at the end of the night from the few that listened.

"Even so. Do you know what that means?"

I shrugged. There wasn't much to know. The stories of seventh sons were always varied, always tragic. Some turned into deer and were hunted and shredded by wolves. Others gambled away their luck. Some spurned old crones who turned into vengeful witches. Their lives were bright, but they were also short.

"The mother of a seventh son will watch their child fall from grace. You've heard those stories I know, but they all start at the birth of the child, even before that the mother is punished for challenging the will of the gods."

"Punished?"

"A seventh son is a powerful omen, a prosperous one, but since there must always be balance, it is also an unlucky one. A seventh son of a seventh son will be strong, clever, handsome—this is a guarantee. Your son could be strong—will be strong."

These were promises I heard before, from the midwife, from my husband. Promises like this meant nothing, couldn't mean anything while those rocks sat outside my home. I didn't want to picture this son that the witch spoke of. "It's just a story."

"You don't believe me?"

"I've been promised these things before."

"Ah, but you've never had a seventh son before." Mirwalda teased. "There are potions I can give you to ensure the child's birth."

"You're not listening to me." I grabbed my basket and tossed out some of the eggs onto the ash-covered table as payment. Two quick steps and I reached the door. My hand gripped the handle before the witch stopped me.

"You say you don't want this child. You also don't want your husband -- I can see it. This birth would solve both of your problems and would leave you a very wealthy woman."

"I didn't say I didn't want the child." I tugged the door handle but the heavy wood refused to open. Finally, I turned back to the witch and said softly. "I don't want the pregnancy. That's different."

"Hmmm…and the husband?" Mirwalda plucked up one of the eggs I'd left on the table. She balanced it on its tip before giving it a deft spin. The egg turned and turned, never wobbling its pace. "How much would you give to have him just fade away?"

Her words stopped me, but then they were meant to. My father warned me that I had chosen poorly, blinded by a young man's bright red hair and charmingly poor background. But I prided myself that at least I had chosen, unlike my friends whose marriages were arranged like chess pieces. Hector wasn't a violent man; we only ever fought with words, short barbed things meant to peck at each other. He would push and I would pull until we'd reach a delicate standoff. Over the years of our marriage, I found it difficult to feel anything besides constant irritation. Hector wandered from one scheme to the next, blaming any failure on the will of the gods. If it were up to him, he'd never make a decision. He'd just wait for the dice to fall the way he wanted them to. There were debts, though Hector never wanted to speak of them.

Mirwalda snatched the egg from its spin and, with one hand, cracked it into her mouth. She slurped it down noisily while beckoning me back over to the table.

Once I settled back into the chair, the witch started speaking again. "You were correct before. This child will bring death, but not yours. As I said, seventh sons of seventh sons are unusually strong. Twice as strong, twice as clever, twice as lucky as the average man. There is a reason for such a thing."

"Magic," I said dully as my hand cradled my pouched-out stomach.

"No. Something old and deeper than magic. I'd also call it a prophecy for lack of a better word, for it's never steered me wrong. *A seventh dynasty ended, a seventh dynasty begun.*

Woe to the mother of a seventh son. Think upon these words. Carefully."

"A dynasty ended." I repeated slowly, going over the verse again in my mind. "Wait…ended?"

"As I said, a seventh son is a powerful being. Such power requires a source." Mirwalda leaned over and squeezed my hand, just like Hector squeezed it days ago. "Take my potion. Keep the fertility idol. Visit the midwife. Endure this. There is no magic I can give you than is stronger than the magic inside of you right now. I promise you, on the eve of the birth, your husband will weaken. The child will grow and strengthen, and your husband will…not."

The words chilled me, but not as much as the rest of the verse that ran through my mind. "And my son, you said this curse…prophecy would affect him too?"

The witch looked confused. "Does it matter? You've had your fill of children, you're tired. I can see it, you love the first. What do you care what becomes of him? He will grow and swell within you, then you will expel him and he'll no longer be yours. But what *will* be yours is the favor of the king's family."

My breath caught. "You've never had a child, have you?"

"Maybe I've had hundreds. Don't presume." Mirwalda glared.

"What if I have the child…but don't want to give him away?" I asked softly, "What if I kept him?"

She snorted in response. "There is always a balance. You came to me this morning. Where did your husband go? Pfft.

Your husband has already informed the king's guard of your health. They will visit whether you want them to or not."

My stomach dropped at the admission. I shouldn't have been shocked or surprised. It was just like Hector to chase whatever sparked his imagination.

"My advice was free, my time is not. And you're wasting it. I've given you all I can, what you do is up to you. Go lay in your birthing bed for eight months, or go throw yourself off a cliff. The choice is yours."

As I grabbed my basket and shakily returned to my feet, Mirwalda shuffled to her kitchen and pulled a vial of green liquid from the dusty shelves. "If you choose to have the child, drink this. It will help ease any pain in bringing the child to term. Three sips everyday. The bottle will refill until the child is born."

She tossed it at me. I grabbed it out of the air, the potion warm and alive in my hands. I remember the times I dragged myself to the cabin, stomach clenching in pain. "Why did you never give me this before?"

"You weren't useful before."

I gripped the vial tightly, sure that it would break. "And now?"

Mirwalda grasped my chin, forcing me to bend until I met her gaze. Her other hand gripped mine, squeezing until the corners of the glass bit into my skin. "This potion is not free. You can bear the child without, but I doubt you would. You fear pain and death, this releases you from that."

She let go and smiled when she saw that I still held the potion.

"You said you didn't want gold?"

"I remember your husband, remember the qualities of his blood. You have that child, I'll know. Once you have the riches, I want the remains."

"The remains?"

She glared. "The body. I want your husband's body. Even a seventh son has a small measure of power, I want that."

I hesitated. If it was prophecy, then it wasn't murder. I couldn't be blamed for the will of the gods. He wanted the child; it was right that he should face the consequences too. Perhaps Hector would be pleased that he was destined for a witch's magic. All the card readings that promised Hector great things, had they all been pointing to this? When I nodded in agreement, Mirwalda had already turned away.

"Leave the bread," she ordered, "and send the next girl in."

***

I gave birth on a Wednesday.

Hector slept through the night, a deep unnatural slumber that had begun only the month before, as I screamed in the kitchen. My eldest, Emma, held my hand and helped bring her brother into the world. With the final push, our kitchen illuminated with glow of a falling star, casting strange shadows onto the vial of potion I kept near. The baby was small, just as small as all the other births. He was born blue, with a shock of black hair atop his still face. My heart froze and broke until the midwife swatted him and the child gave a sharp cry. His eyes opened quickly, too quickly; the midwife gasped, already a dark brown instead of blue. I could see my features in his small face.

He was mine. My Oliver.

Emma didn't want to touch him, but I found it difficult to let Oliver of out my arms. When I held him, his legs kicked out like he was already itching to run. I thought about hiding him when the King's guard arrived, tricking them by handing over another's child, but Mirwalda was true to her word, the only other babe in our village was the Miller's daughter.

The King's guard arrived at the week's end with Mirwalda at their side. She touched my hand and I froze, letting the guards push past me. Any of the lies I prepared caught in my throat, unable to be voiced. My son wailed as they took him away in a wet-nurse's arms. In Oliver's stead they left a bag of gold, and a promise that a new bag would appear in exchange for every year of his life.

My husband still slept in the bedroom, Charles curled at his feet like a cat. I barely saw the boy during the brief time I had Oliver. Hector's normally deep breath, grew labored and rattled louder with each passing day. It wouldn't be long before Mirwalda returned to claim him.

Above him a new crack spidered along the length of our patched ceiling.

The Fox Witch

J. Motoki

J. Motoki graduated from the College of
Creative Studies at University of CA,
Santa Barbara with a BA in literature/
creative writing. She is writer and
library clerk who lives in Colorado with
her husband and two cats. She is also the
Short Story Editor of Coffin Bell Journal
and the Strange Editor of Rune Bear.
Her works have been published or are
forthcoming in Black Hare Press, The
Other Stories Podcast (Hawk & Cleaver),
Coffin Bell Journal, and others. You can
find her lurking on Twitter @J_Motoki.

"In the depths of the mountains,
Whom was it for the aged mother snapped
One twig after another?
Heedless of herself
She did so
For the sake of her son."

—Buddhist Allegory

The old woman awoke in a bed of snow. She lay on her side, curled like a centipede, with ice brushed over her kimono, rough and thinning from long summers.

"Why dress her in layers?" Kesa had protested the night before, as her husband fretted over his mother's apparel. "Why dress her at all? Those clothes will keep our children alive. Granny Orin will not need them in the mountains."

Orin's son, a quiet and nervous man, who never questioned the authority of his wife, looked at her as if a stranger had appeared before him.

"Would you have me carry my mother without clothes?" Tatsu asked, his tone mild but his eyes holding hers. She was the first to look away for once. "My mother will be comfortable to the best of my ability—to the very end."

Orin had smiled in the corner near the fire—altercations between her son and daughter-in-law were enjoyable but rare—and hugged Shuya, her youngest grandson, to her breast. In the morning, of course, she left her winter kimono, her blanket, her wool socks and rice straw sandals. How could she not? Her three grandchildren clutched at her hem. She could see the bones under their rags, fragile as bird wings. If the winter grew worse, her family would chew on the braided straw of the sandals to fill their sunken bellies, and they would need everything they could scrounge to push back the cold.

Orin shifted in the snow, rolling onto her back, her arms outspread, eyes on the stars draped across the southern sky. Never in her life had she lain in a bed as soft as this one. And the view—did they have as magnificent a view at Edo castle? White below and black above, and the pregnant moon and all her spinning courtiers turning night into day.

If this was dying, then dying was wonderful. Even the whispers of the dead felt as natural—as inconsequential—as the snowfall over her body.

Get up.

A whisper. It came from the three stones that had for centuries served as a shrine to the mountain spirits, the honorable dead, the ones who sacrificed their lives for kin. The tri-stones marked the place as *Shintaisan*, the sacred mountain.

Do not look to the sky, little one. There is nothing of value up there.

A low moan punctuated the strange remark. Orin looked beyond the stones and cried out. She started to her feet. There in the snow slumped the body of her neighbor and childhood friend. Had she not seen Aki carried out of the village the week before, the very day he turned seventy? Aki's son was not as strong as Tatsu, and he had struggled under the weight of his father—who was as withered as a bundle of firewood.

Aki lifted his head slowly, and his eyes were two black embers in the bottom of a fire. He opened his mouth to speak, but she heard nothing, nothing over the whispering of thousands of voices.

Now she could see the shadows of people in the clearing, standing with their arms around their bellies as if holding in their insides. The old woman pushed herself to her knees, sat in a stance of respect to her friend.

Come here little one.

That voice. It was not Aki who was speaking to her.

"I am old," the old woman snapped at the night. "And not little by any means. Why do you call to me like a child?"

Something laughed in the darkness, melodic and nearer than before.

You are little in the eyes of the mountain.

The old woman stood, slowly, brushing snow from her kimono and pulling a small, yellowing bone from her hair. Then she made her way through the skeletons of cypress trees, calligraphy strokes against the snow. The branches plucked at her hem, caught her hair. Otherwise, neither the forest or the shadows bothered her. She walked among them, trying not to stare, to an archway weaved from living branches. Orin had to bend low to the ground, as if bowing, to enter. The high neck of her kimono slipped from her neck and she shivered, feeling uncertain for the first time.

"Please enter," a low, musical voice said.

Orin stared. The alcove beyond the green wood had expanded, because surely it looked larger than when she had approached. Inside the space was a low table. Nearby, a fire sat crackling on the dirt. Hanging over it was an iron cauldron, bubbling with spring-green liquid.

There was a woman, stirring the contents of the cauldron. Orin could make out the blue tints in her waist-length hair, the silver of her silk-worm kimono. A pale white light emanated from her skin, glowing, as if she had been infused by moonlight. Her eyes were pale and pupil less. She looked straight into the approaching old woman as if she were not as blind as she appeared.

"Who are you?" Orin said.

"I guard the Gates of the *Shintaisan*," the woman said, "and guide those who are abandoned here."

"Am I dead then?" Orin asked. She felt as alive as she had in her youth, strong from working the rice fields.

The shining woman did not answer. She stirred the cauldron with a ladle of polished bone. Inscriptions wove up and down the handle. Orin walked as if in a dream, as if her feet did not come into contact with the ground. If something were to chase her, a malevolent spirit or one of these pour souls keening in the wind, she would run in place as if in water.

The woman gestured to the low table. They both sat with their legs unfolding beneath them on the earthen floor. The woman offers Orin a cup of tea with both hands.

"Please partake," she said graciously.

Orin accepted the tea bowl with her right hand and placed it in her left. She had forgotten the traditional etiquette. It had been a long time since a tea ceremony—since any ceremony. She would have to rely on the memories of her fingers. They sipped together. The tea was hot and bitter. Orin was surprised to discover that, even in death, tea could still burn the tip of her tongue.

"That is incorrect," the woman said, her white gaze studying Orin's hands. "Tradition dictates turning the tea clockwise so that it faces away from you. You drink the tea in a few sips before placing it back on the table."

"Tradition dictates that tea be boiled from a teapot," Orin replied. She watched the bubbling mixture in the cauldron, the steam rising. She had forgotten the ways her mother taught her.

Feeling rebellious, Orin slurped the tea with savage pleasure and smacked her lips loudly. Strong, bitter. Thick as bone broth.

"I once knew of a royal court who serve their guests ten cups of tea to begin," said the woman. "Then another ten. And another. Until it becomes a game in which the guest cannot refuse the drink and the host cannot stop pouring, until one of them admits defeat."

Orin belched, a fluid sound that made the woman crease her lips in disgust. Somewhere in the distance, the spirits of the dead laughed softly.

"I was raised in the most isolated village in the world," Orin said, at last, when she had drained the last dregs in her cup. "What do I care for the customs of cities or royal courts?"

The younger woman studied her.

"Yes, of course. Your village has far more interesting traditions, don't they?"

The old woman said nothing.

"Abandoned by your village, by your only son," the woman said, insistent. "I ask each of you your journey through the gates. Why do you all insist upon isolation and poverty? Why not seek other places to live?"

"You wouldn't understand," Orin said. "Whatever you are. With all due respect. Where would we go? Everything we have ever known is here, tucked away in the hills and hollows with summer droughts and winter freezes. And still we survive. Our village has survived."

"It has," the woman said. "And at what cost?"

Those white, pupilless eyes seemed to be laughing at Orin, although the woman's face was expressionless.

"We survive because we know our place. Our duties," the old woman said to fill the silence. She was helpless to prevent the defensive notes in her voice. "It is an honor to offer ourselves to the spirits of the mountain. We scrabble for survival every day, but when it comes to protecting the village, we each do our part."

This time the woman laughed outright.

"How noble," she said.

Orin drew herself upright, her curved spine protesting.

"I have lived for seventy years," she said. "The oldest in the village. And I have lived so long, despite my friends being carried off into the mountains, because I am useful. I make clothes from wool, know which roots are medicine and which are poison, keep the sacred tales. It was this past year that was my downfall."

She had caught a cold and never recovered. Something had happened to her hands, and they trembled. And she was no longer able to pick up a needle and thread, or prepare meals.

For the first time, Orin felt doubt. The face of her son who clutched her hands, and every step that carried them up the mountain had seemed to beg for forgiveness. Tatsu had always been more sensitive than his peers, always clung to her skirt as they tended the rice paddies, hated to be parted with her for more than a moment. She had bartered her ceramic teapot and cups, passed down from her own grandmother, in order to secure a marriage for him. Her beloved heirlooms for the proud and hardened Kesa.

It was a testament to her industrious nature that the entire village turned out in the snow that morning, in the bitter cold, to bid her farewell. How different it was for Aki the week before, carried on the back of the son-in-law he despised. Aki's own sons had died years ago and only a few faces braved the ice to send him off.

It was colder this year. Less forgiving. The wind reddened their cheeks and frosted eyelashes. And yet they came, husks of the people she loved.

The people of the village bowed to her. The village elder thanked her. She looked at their pinched faces. The sunken sockets of the young ones. So many children dead that winter—

Orin did not fear. She held her head up high. Tatsu was expressionless when he bowed to the villagers and then to her, before kneeling in the snow. She climbed on the wooden seat that was secured to Tatsu's back by braided rice straw straps. It was tradition.

"Have some more tea," the woman said gently. They were back in the green wood, in the land beyond the shrine. The woman took her bone ladle, the possibility that it was made from the parts of someone she knew suddenly occurred to Orin, and brought forth more tea from her strange cauldron.

This time the tea was a dark viscous liquid, a green that was almost black. Orin recoiled from it and held her breath. She scarcely looked at it as she drank, and managed to stifle her cries at the ensuing scorch in her throat.

The wind blew, rattling the tea sets. It was a chilling wind, full of dark tree breaths and bones beneath the ice. Then the woods were around Orin so fast it took away her breath. The mountain was bare and the stones glowed. She was alone—alone in a blue twilight, when stars were less friendly. She gasped.

There was a man.

He struggled on the incline, his feet tramping through the snow, his breath like fire smoke. A person was strapped to his back. A person unknown to her.

The man stopped at the stones and knelt. A small figure tumbled to the snow and clawed forward with his arms. Then Orin put her hands to stifle the sound trying to escape her lips, because the man with the chair was her son, and the figure in the snow was her eldest grandson, Shuya. Older, twisted, but she knew him instantly. He had the same curious sparrow-tilt of his head, looking around at the open space. His father gently arranged him near the stones, sank to his knees by him and bowed his head.

"Your grandson is brave," the woman said. "Look—he shows no

fear, even as his father leaves him. He knows his place and his duty. He knows a crippled boy is of no use to a starving village in winter."

"No," Orin said, reaching out instinctively for the boy. He looked so small and alone in the snow. "No, he is strong. He is whole. He has the most energy out of his siblings."

"He did," the woman said. "And then he did not."

The boy tumbled down the rocks in search of game. Shattering his leg, irreparable. Screams. Her son and Kesa looking woodenly at the damage. No one cried in the village.

"No," Orin whispered, her mouth dry.

"The old, the weak, the un-whole," the woman said. "And—"

A woman with a moving bundle shivering in the night. She kissed the infant before lying him on the ground by the stones. Her hands clasped together, she bowed to the spirits.

The village shrinks, the wind whispers, came the voice. Orin blinked. Where was she? Was she the glowing rocks, the dead eye of the moon? And still the droughts come and rob them of water, the winters come and rob them of life.

"No," Orin said, louder. It had never been this bad. Not in a hundred generations. Children were cared for over all else—they were given the food; the adults went without. This could not be the future.

Now she saw the village, the thatched straw roofs. She saw the worst of it, the frozen excrement, the faces of familiar people twisted in cruelty, stupidity. The vacant blank agonized expressions of beasts. Saw the old people carried in droves up the mountain.

You can stop this.

That whisper again filling her head.

Orin saw herself, small and wizened, on the back of her only son and surrounded by friends and family. Their eyes gleamed and they looked eager, viciously eager, like crows picking apart a frozen carcass. And Kesa with her pinched cheeks, wearing Orin's own cloak as she shivered in the snow and she looked triumphant. Even the children laughed as if it were all a game. Orin clenched her fists, nails cutting her palms.

"I will tear them all down," Orin said in a voice not her own. It was a feral noise, a growl. Behind her, the glowing woman towered, nine fox tails waving behind her like a fan. The woman's face was longer than ever—all sharp angles.

The woman waved a hand.

"Look," she said.

Orin stood on top of the mountain overlooking the village. Rage filled her at the sight. The people within who slept easily in her absence, the ones allowed to live. She howled into the night. Silent shadows padded in the snow and foxes emerged from their dens, surrounding her, awaiting her command. Orin raised her arm.

And froze.

Hovering at the edge of her periphery, barely visible, stood the white figure of Aki. When she turned, he looked at her with charcoal eyes, his mouth open and soundless. Orin felt hot all over—her skin exuded sweat that chilled, a fever breaking.

"My throat is dry," Orin said suddenly.

A flash of annoyance crossed the glowing woman's face, but she ladled more liquid into her cup. This was weaker tea, watery brown, the way Orin used to make it in her hut. Barley and roasted rice, fresh from the fields. A peasant's brew, rough but filling. Orin threw back her head and drained it in moments.

The world changed.

Orin was on her son's back again, in the wooden chair used to haul the village old up the mountain. She brushed a dead leaf from his graying hair.

Above, the skies rumbled and darkened with incoming storms, but it was not snowing yet. Orin thanked the spirits for that, and prayed for his safe journey home. She reached and snapped the brittle branches from an overhanging tree and cast them in the white snow, leaving a marker for her son. If they hurried, he would have light enough to guide him down again. They walked in silence, the crunch of snow deafening under Tatsu's tabi boots.

Orin put her arms around her son, hugged him closely, smelled his familiar scent. His body flickered, revealing the table before her and the dark alcove of trees. The glowing woman blinked in and out of her vision.

No, she would not join the foxes in the hunt.

Orin breathed deeply, gathered herself. She smashed her cup against the table, where it shattered into splinters. The glowing woman screamed, a wild and animalistic sound rising, accompanied by the deafening yips and howls of her foxes. Orin threw her hands over her head to keep out the sound. A gust of wind rose around her, blinding her, erasing the trees and the table and the glowing woman like a stifled fire.

Silence. She was on her back in the snow and the sky was clear.

She knew this unfriendly ice covered the bones and fragments of her village generations, and it was comforting that so many had gone before her. Orin drowsed, and suddenly it was dawn. There was a glow on the horizon, red as a fox coat in autumn.

When the moon was high, Orin slept once more, spinning through those dreams which guard the door to death.

Bone to Bleeding Bone

Sarah McGill

Sarah McGill has published fantasy short stories in Giganotosarus, Luna Station Quarterly, Metaphorosis, and elsewhere. Her favorite time and place is post-revolution France at the height of the Death Cabarets, mostly because the bohemians really did walk their lobsters in the rose gardens and pretend hydropathes were Canadian animals whose feet were made into drinking glasses.

When I was old enough to bleed, my step-sister pushed me out the window of a tall tower. Except, I was the step-sister, not her. I was the sneer-mouthed child who came under her portcullis in a vermillion carriage to sleep under new covers, in someone else's bed. She was the dimple-faced daughter who only wanted to mourn her mother and cry under the wisteria arbors.

I pitied Nourie when I first saw her, her face blotched in red and white with silent tears still dripping down her cheeks – as if she'd forgotten how to stop crying. "No more black," my mother said when introductions were over, instead of an easier *how do you do?* "Don't wear it anymore."

Nourie curtsied and cried harder. I leaned down to pick the purple bell vine from the well and wound it around my wrist like a bracelet.

"No more crying either," my mother said.

The bracelet fell off when we went inside and I twisted my heel on the flower to paint the threshold lilac. I wasn't surprised by what my mother had said, but my new sister looked back at us like we were ghouls. She looked at us no more fondly when, that night, Mother told the story of the old king who died on his throne and gave commands until his lips rotted away.

In the morning Nourie wore a white kirtle, sewn with pearls. I think she wore it so she could tell us how much she hated pearls. "They're like tongues or hearts, stripped out of a cracked body." She shivered when she touched them, as if they were still slimy with decaying muscle and saltwater.

Mother cut her strawberries into halves. "Cutting out a heart is more difficult than snapping an oyster. But you can eat a heart and gain something from its owner."

Nourie made a horrible face.

I examined our new dishes, which were lightly painted with a pink rose garden, and asked what *di Rosaio* meant. I looked at my sister because it was, after all, her name. I'd only been given it yesterday. But she huffed and twisted in her chair until I couldn't see her face.

"It means 'of the rose tree,'" my mother said, pulling my hand away as I tried to uncover one of the painted roses that had been drowned in a sheen of blueberry juice.

"Is there a rose tree here?"

"There are rose trees everywhere," Nourie broke in. "What else would you have in a garden?"

"Thistles and dandelions." I grinned and snuck a drop of blueberry juice onto my finger and into my mouth.

"You don't know anything." Nourie hopped off her chair and refused to be called back.

Mother stood and kept pace behind the girl, holding her gold and white embroidered skirt off the floor. I wondered if she was going to make sure Nourie didn't throw herself down somewhere to sob. When I cried, Mother said, "I expect more of you." She said it again and kept saying it until I could take a deep breath and say it back.

"I expect more of myself. I expect more of myself."

With no one to watch me, I slipped from my chair and went to find the garden.

Out a back door and past the wall, I found the Queen's Garden. It was filled with copses of rose trees, standing like rings of mourners clad in silk. The roses hung heavy as bee-stung lips, achingly red and pale white as a stretched neck. Beneath the dead Queen's window, the roses were the dull pink of an atrium. They were beautiful and wonderful and I wished I were as pretty.

I snapped a rose from its woody branch and put it in my mouth. Its strings caught in my teeth and it tasted bitter. I sucked the thorny stem and caught the blood with my knuckles.

When Mother found me, she told me not to stain my clothes. Nourie, sucking in breaths so deep she looked like she would faint, twisted her face. But she couldn't glare without risking tears again.

That evening she said she wouldn't share her roses. "Don't you know they were my mother's?" she shouted.

She tore the pearls from her dress and threw them at me, wrenching the rose from my mouth so it cut into my tongue. I hit her hard across the face.

I was sorry as she fell. I wanted to tell her the roses were beautiful and I needed them too. I wanted her to smile and say she understood, and would I like to share them with her? Instead I caught the blood with my cupped hands and ran to Mother, who tucked a kerchief under my chin until I stopped spitting red. All the while I huffed and gasped and didn't cry.

***

In the hallway beneath a window, I found the pearls, gathered like rainwater in the corner. I picked one up and put it in my mouth. It tasted of lye water.

Mother found me that afternoon, spitting the opalescent rocks at Nourie in the Garden. They left dark spots on her dress, trails of spit like snail slime. I stopped when I saw Mother, begrudgingly guilty, but Nourie still fled into her arms, squirming and twitching. Mother caught her thoughtlessly. I kicked a dead rose head, the petals bursting like a paper heart around my foot. Mother smiled and told me the pearls were perfect.

When a prince in cobalt regalia and milky trim came courting, Mother made me hide a pearl under my tongue, to let slip later, as if some virtue between my lungs and liver expressed itself most keenly through productions of virginal-white stones. She smiled big as a behemoth when my greeting was punctuated by the pearl falling into the prince's hand. I think the only reason he didn't propose a match that instant was because Mother promised I wouldn't marry until I bled.

Though, watching him clutch the pearl, close-lipped smiling like a little boy, I couldn't remember why it had been important for Mother to make that promise. Especially when he decided even a pearl-mouth wasn't worth the wait and packed his retinue like bolts of silk and lace. I watched him leave with crossed arms, hoping the road would split and swallow him up.

Mother decided after that to cast my sister as the saucier of us. Nourie began pinching her lips red and taking rubies under her tongue. Her suitors did make eyes at her when, during a particularly crystalline ballad, she let the ruby fall between her silk slippers. She was particularly apt at dropping them upon a man's shoe, so he had to kneel before her to retrieve it. They thought it was like a kiss between them, secret and sweet and with a little teeth. But she thought it was stupid.

For a while, Nourie and I made friends over deciding that Mother was completely ridiculous. I might like being called a Rose Tree Sister, as if I had the sort of beauty that could be compared to roses and pearls. I might even sometimes enjoy how a minister or chamberlain turned up his eyebrows at me as they had never done before the pearls, but it was impossible not to be embarrassed too. Nourie didn't need the rubies to make people look at her like that.

One night Nourie crept into my bed, tugging on my hair until I sat up and snapped, "What?"

She lay with her hair spread across my pillow, the moonlight lighting up her eyes like stars. "There's a king coming tomorrow. He lives in a black castle and his garden is full of hemlock and nightshade. He wants to meet you."

"Everyone who comes to San Viano wants to meet one of us."

"You should pretend to choke on the pearl and then spit it horribly onto his jacket sleeve." She grinned.

"He'll be angry."

"It'll be funny. Please. I want to see you do it."

So I did.

Nourie nearly rolled off her seat when I vomited the pearl and a glob of mucus into the king's hair while he was kissing the back of my hand. I'd eaten duck that night and I imagine it smelled of stomach bile and duck oil. The king started like a rabbit drawn out of the bush by hounds and looked at me in disgust. I wanted desperately to tell him I was sorry.

I tried to tell Mother later that I had just about swallowed that nasty rock. But I've never been a good liar.

To make me feel better, Nourie lined her mouth in rubies and when she smiled at the next prince, she looked like a monster. "I thought if one ruby was charming, five would be simply dazzling," she told Mother.

"Dazzling indeed," Mother said. But Nourie was much more convincing than me. So it was me who was slapped on the wrist and fed rye bread and old applesauce for a week. Our shared crime made me giddy and I grinned fiercely when Nourie praised my part in it. But I felt like a dog in my room and I wished Nourie had asked me to do something pretty.

Nourie quickly fell in love with her ruby teeth – or, perhaps, it would be better to say she fell in love with the way that prince tumbled over himself and refused to stay in San Viano another moment. But she couldn't quite live up to them. She made faces at dukes and earls, until they asked if she was feeling quite alright. She tried to scare servants by jumping out of corners at night, until they asked if she was still a child. I once found her howling out her window, into the apple orchards and rose garden, and I laughed so hard she slapped me. I didn't mean to make her angry. But she sounded more like a startled grouse than a wolf.

"How do you think you'll scare anyone?" I told her. "You're too pretty. People aren't afraid of pretty girls."

She beat her fist against the stone wall until her knuckles bruised. "I'm not. I'm not too pretty."

I knew she believed me, even as she spit out the window. She braided white roses into her hair and hung fresh buds off her wrist. She smiled impulsively and smelled of rosewater. When she cried, which happened less and less with the passing years, she always ended up in the arms of whoever was closest. Some pig-headed prince once told Nourie he wasn't surprised she'd stopped mourning her mother so quickly – the woman had been a hideous ghoul. For his callousness, he found a princess wrapped up in his arms, sobbing against his chest and blubbering too much to call him a stinking dog. I would have, if he'd not left before Nourie would tell me what had brought her to my room with red eyes. "Don't tell Mother," she said as she tried to hide the blotches.

But I was a step-sister. I was born to snarl, to have too-ruddy cheeks, to know just how to make Nourie feel like she was stupid and completely unimportant. When she snuck away from lessons to spend an afternoon with Mother, I was sure to follow after and take up Mother's time. It wasn't Mother's fault. She tried to be fair to both of us, but I was her flesh and blood and when I took her hands, she had no eyes for Nourie. I was sure, too, to often ask after cutting out hearts and then never look repulsed. Such things still made Nourie squirm.

Nourie cupped her hand as it turned purple and black, her back to me. "You have to teach me how to howl, then."

I thought of saying no, so she could not have all of my things. But I wanted more to be part of her schemes, whatever they might be, and so I said yes.

***

When Nourie began to bleed, she decided to bring San Viano to its knees. She asked me to do it, because even though I'd taught her how to howl, she could never do it like me. And I did, because she wanted me to, even if I didn't.

I cut open the tips of my fingers and smeared blood on bottle-glass windows, crystal goblets, and across Mother's dress like a ghoul. I spoke to strangers in gibberish tongues until a stable boy insisted I show him my mouth to prove I wasn't a tongue-less beast. I licked my lips and grinned with all my teeth. In the autumn, as the roads ran red with falling leaves, I shredded roses across the carpets. Soon Mother confined me to my room, locked away from dances and dinners and visitors.

With the years I grew, hungry and lean, boney shoulders pressed against the ceiling as I cracked my nails upon the floor.

I filled up the castle with my absence as Nourie never could. I heard them whispering through the walls. I saw them looking over their shoulder, like I was the ghost around the corner. I spit blood from my window and if it stained someone's skin, they fled San Viano, casting charms and prayers over their shoulders. I did it because I was good at it, but the terrified looks made me cower.

When Nourie visited, I laughed at her. She'd told me to be a monster and I didn't know how to stop. I called her sweet and honey and darling. I told her she was just a rose bud. I told her her mother had been born an apple blossom, pink and already dying. Over time, she stopped visiting. I saw no one and I chewed at the walls, waiting for them to crack.

Mother visited and shook her head. "I taught you better than this. People are scared of you. You can't do anything if people are scared of you."

I didn't know what else to do. Nourie had forgotten how to cry, as I had never learned to do. She didn't wear black and she was beautiful. She could creep up men's spines and wrap her fingers around their throats as though it were a sign of love. No one would let me do that.

"You told me not to cry and no one would know if I meant to slit their throat or curl up in their arms."

"Everyone knows you want to slit their throat."

I waited for Nourie to tell me I could stop, so we might once again sit down as sisters and giggle over the virility of visiting nobles and mock Mother's passion for blood and jewels. I waited for her to come and teach me how to be good at something else, like smiling or wearing roses in my hair. But while I waited for her, she became jealous of me.

When she understood how I had caged the castle up with my fingers as she couldn't, she stole Mother's key and let me out. She took me by the hand and up we went, up and up so I thought we would reach the clouds before we reached the top. I stared at her rose-bound hair and waited breathlessly for her smile. But when she looked back at me, I could see in the way her eyes grew wide that she still wanted her sister to be monstrous and gaping.

In that pinnacle of rooms, Nourie showed me a mirror. It hung heavy against the wall, cracking the stone fixing.

Her fingers wrung my wrist until it burned. I stared at her through the mirror and I thought she would reach into my throat and tear my heart from its nest of skin and bone. She stood taller than me and I shriveled like a rotted apple.

"Sister," she said, looking at the sweaty flush across my neck.

"Who between us is fairest of them all? Do you think you are more beautiful than me?"

She pulled her fingers across my cheek, hard enough to strip away the skin. Her nails chafed my jaw and the sweat of her palms was thick with rosewater. I didn't know what she wanted to hear. I think I was supposed to hug her like a rose vine and tell her I would teach her to speak in gibberish and spit blood.

But I saw how she was trying to shame me, with that one thing she'd always had and I never would. After I had been her monster for so many years.

"I am." My breath rasped against my lips, creaking and dry. In the mirror I saw the faint scars on my lips where I'd sucked rose stems. I saw the ends of my teeth that were stained with boar gristle and blood. All of my body snarled and keened against the mirror. "I am more beautiful than you."

With her rose-cut ruby ring piercing my back, she pushed me from the window into the river down below.

***

I fell through a sea of rose petals and apple blossoms, a milky ocean above a river of ink. I gasped as the river buried me, running through me like a thorn. Upon rocks and river banks, among pearlwort and rushes, the river threw me. It pushed itself into my throat and ripped it full of holes. I bled until I thought I would run dry.

When the sun set, I washed up at the edge of Mother's kingdom. The rose trees gathered around me, waiting for me to die. Petals fell across my fingers. I looked back at San Viano and shrieked. The rose trees trembled, waxy leaves gusting away on the wind. I wanted to drag myself on my belly to the citadel and show

Nourie my bleeding mouth and ruined throat. I dug my hands through the petals as if I could make her break by ripping the roses along their veins. The sky ran red as blood in water and I couldn't come to my feet.

I struggled and slipped and screamed in the mud. I raged against Nourie and blamed her for everything. If her mother hadn't died, this wouldn't have happened. If she hadn't wanted me to be a monster, I could have snuck away under a prince's cloak and learned what else you grew in a garden. I had sneered and pinched and called her names. But she never thought I was good enough.

I lurched towards a rose tree, and fell. I cracked my skull upon a rock and out fell seven beautiful pearls – white as bone. They lay among the blossoms, wet with dark blood.

There on the river bank, I would have crowned my pearl-children with apple crowns and rose lips. Then they might be princess too, beautiful, laughing children that ran through the orchards in lacey gowns and never knew what it meant to scream into an empty sky.

But my lungs were filled with mud and the rot of fish and water birds. I tasted skin and heartstrings. Onto my pearl-children I coughed mucus and clots of black blood. They smelled of bile and the butcher's block.

I sank into the mud, among alder roots and oyster mushrooms, breathing so hard I thought I would faint.

***

"Pretty feathers, do you think you're more beautiful than me?" I asked the birds, grey-tailed herons and ruby-eyed mallards. They flapped their wings and honked among the buzz of flies.

They tossed oily water across their backs and ate the jewelweed under the water.

"You aren't. You're only birds. You're muscle and feather and ugly squawks." But as I watched a heron strike its wings against the water, sending up drops of blue water, even the heron was more beautiful than me. I turned my head and blood spilled across my eyes. Bottle flies buzzed up and then resettled on my legs.

"Come here so I can cut a hole in your chest and skewer your heart on my nails. If I eat a bird heart whole, it will make me slender and bright-eyed." My eyes stung. "Maybe that's what monsters do, but if I eat a dove heart, at least I will be fair and kind as well."

My children found me first. They came at night like wolves, carrying milk snakes and musk turtles in their mouths. They scratched long nails through the apple trees and tore up the wet ground. They gathered to laugh, pointing at the scar cut deep into my skull where the hair had fallen away. "The river didn't want your ugly skeleton. It retched you up. You're slimy with its sick."

I caught the river bank in my hand and my fingers bled on rocks and fish teeth. I wanted to shout something back at them that would prove them wrong. But my body ached and I had drained all my blame on Nourie.

"Covered in blood. Covered in blood." They chattered and sang and howled at the Milk Moon. "Dead. Dead. Dead."

"Night-ghouls," I called them, though my heart wasn't in it. "Rot guts. River-stained."

They crept forward and put their fingers through the holes in my skull. They hooted at the cold and bit the blood off their palms, spitting it into the grass. "Mother." They cracked each other's arms as they pounded on the ground. "Monster." I retched at the old smell of fish. "Who threw you down and picked you up? Who filled you up with holes? Princess?" They struck each other's heads.

I shoved them away and wrapped my fingers around my temple. "At least I'm not so hideous as you. Come closer and I will crack your pearl hearts with my teeth."

They shrieked and pulled on their lips. "Good luck, good luck. They're buried deep. Deeper than your heart." They pranced forward and poked at the purple skin filled with pooling blood until I snatched at them and they rolled away.

"We went to the castle today. We knocked at the door, but they wouldn't let us in. They looked at us and gagged, covering their eyes and plugging their noses. They poured hot oil onto our heads and we squealed." They parted the burned hair at their scalp and the skin under it was red and bleeding, falling away under their fingers. "'Nourie, Nourie,' we called. 'Come out and put rubies in our mouths. We will spit pearls into yours and show you how to be a monster.' Have you heard, mother dear? Do you know? She's to be married. She'll ride away on a rose-colored mare and teach her husband the secret of her rubies. She'll be a queen then and queens and monsters alike eat hearts."

I grew silent.

"She whispered down, as if she thought we wouldn't hear, 'Where is my sister? Can I still find her and speak to her? Tell me what happened.' 'You did!' we told her. We threw oyster shells at her and they shattered against her walls."

"Fine." I didn't want to hear about Nourie. I'd already screamed and pounded my fists against the ground and spit all my anger across her petals. If my children wanted to be monsters, they could do it away from my hearing. I didn't need to hear any more of the world or what it thought of me. I only wanted to be a rose tree, with roses red as a blush and leaves as prettily bound as Nourie's hair.

They screeched up at the sky and fled, leaving me among the muck and swollen water. I stared after them and their stretched, black eyes. I was glad for the silence. But I thought too, if I had teeth the length of theirs, I would have run them along Nourie's walls too.

***

My sister found me second. I lay between arrow-petaled laurels and papery dying reeds, swollen milky white and sticky with the liquid that had spilled from my ears and mouth. She strode through the olive ferns and dying rose trees and stood over me as beautifully as a Queen. She looked at me as though she had never known me. I tried to show her the same contempt, but I smelled the rosewater and wine cellars, the sun-dusty halls and smoky fire and I remembered how we had once been princesses, so grand that we filled up the hallways with our reaching arms and greedy mouth. I wanted to touch her, but my body had gone stiff in the night.

In her finely polished fingers she held an apple, as red as a rose. "There are monsters in the Garden," she said. "They shriek up at the stone walls and send themselves into a frenzy, tearing up rose bushes and apple trees. Yesterday, they ate a herd of sheep and beheaded a great-horned goat." She knotted her skirts prettily at her knee and crouched beside me. The earth, damp with my blood, seeped into her shoes.

"They came calling for me." Her lip quivered and she blinked several times, tilting her chin up at the sky. "Is it stupid, I thought it was that king—my husband? My husband now. He has a loud voice; he can bellow through the whole castle. I thought he'd come to visit. I ran to the window, past the guards. And then I heard the cackling and screaming. They were laid out in the oil, screeching as they melted." She put out a hand like she meant to cup my cheek and then pulled back, putting her thumb to the corner of her mouth. "Do you know I'm a Queen now?"

"I've heard queens are monsters," I said.

"I've heard step-sisters are too." She touched my smallest finger bone, bleached white as a pearl.

"If you wait long enough my children will come back and eat you whole."

She looked over her shoulder and it may have been worry or envy. "My husband is fond of the rubies. Every now and again I must surprise him with a ruby clattering on the floor like a bone. I stare at them and wonder why I ever found them silly. He and Mother insisted on it at the marriage. I was going to kiss him and drop it into his mouth. It would have been cute. Maybe even beautiful. But I cut my tongue on the stupid thing during the vows. I could feel the blood welling up in my mouth, and I kissed him anyway. By the end of it there was blood on both of our faces. I wish you'd been there to laugh at it. But it was just horrible." She picked up the end of my finger where the ligaments had just begun to rot away and snapped free the bone.

"He doesn't have roses around his palace. It's cloaked in night-shade and hemlock and it's so dark. Do you remember him? He came for you before. You would have known what to do with him and his Garden. You would tear the flowers with your teeth and strip them with your nails until they were too afraid to hurt you. But I think it's going to eat me. Or kill me." She tightened her hands desperately together, clutching my finger bone to her breast. "Mother said you gain something from a person, if you eat their heart." Her mouth pulled taunt and she nodded sharply.

She took a knife from her sleeve and cut open my chest, from neck to hip. I squealed like a pig on a butcher's block, a ghoul under a knight's dagger. Meticulously she peeled away the skin and laid it out across the water and mud.

Out of the cavity of my body, she tore my heart. I bled for her. I bled red and ochre and mauve until her hands were slick and hot. All the veins and muscles between my ribs spilled across her knees. My stomach broke open and the whole of me cracked in two.

"What would you do with a heart anyway?" she said as it leaked blood across her sleeves. "You never used it." She squeezed her eyes shut. "But I have another for you." Into the debris of broken ribs at the center of my chest, she nestled the apple and covered it over with sinew and black, fatty muscle.

And then she left me there, fleeing with the smells of San Viano. I screamed after her and river water fell in streams from my eyes.

***

My children returned that night, snuffling like pigs in search of truffles. I could feel the apple already rotting inside me, the flesh falling into pieces under the slow trickle of my blood.

"You must be dead," they said. "There are too many pieces for you to be alive."

They muttered between each other and shuffled towards me.

They pawed at my flesh, picking up pieces of skin and bone. "You've no heart at all. An apple tossed between your ribs to root you to the earth and fill you with poison."

"At least it is of a shape and color with a heart. Your hearts might be pretty, but they're stained in rot and bile." My gut ached and I felt as sore as the first night I lay on the river bank.

"How much is your heart worth? We've seen the market walls and the shepherds entering the cities. We've smelled the muck of chopped hooves hung to dry and the autumn harvest spilled on the ground in seeds and apple juices. Is a heart worth as much as a pearl?"

"Your pearls are black and ugly. Anything would be worth more than them. I hope when Nourie eats my heart, her face falls off her bones. I hope it bloats her with such bright red blood that her womb splits open and she bleeds out down her thighs. She can't fill up the castle; only monsters make castles clamor with noise – the noise of swords and spears and questing." Hot tears ran down my sagging flesh.

"Can you fill a castle?" It was the first time I heard them lower their voices. They spoke with wonder, almost longing. They gathered around me, bruised hands folded across their filthy laps. "Can you break the rose trees and scatter the petals? Will you burst the apples and rot the blossoms?"

I looked at my children, their skin putrid and crawling with maggots. They grinned wide at me with broken teeth and red gums. "Yes. I can." And I wanted to. I wanted to destroy the Garden and rake claws across the rose trees until they withered and died. I had no care any more about the ways of the world.

***

Three poisoned seeds lay beneath my rotted muscle. They took to the dirt of me and by spring a sapling had grown up from my chest. By the end of summer, it stood tall as I once had, sick buds drooping from the branches.

The maggots left my rotted flesh and I became mushroom-grown and bark-swollen. Alder roots grew through my knuckles and orange-capped swamp beacons swelled on my cheek. The cellophane mushrooms gathered in my brittle hair and led like a deadly path away into the glassy water.

I watched the leaves and sunk into the ground. The apple tree's roots grew through my ribs and bound me bone to bone like capillaries. My roots stretched out through the Garden and gripped the trees. Around me the yellow and red roses drooped, the petals curling grey as ash. The air smelled of apples, sweet and tart.

I burst the apples and rotted the leaves. I sucked in the air and replaced it with my breath. I raked through the Garden until I had bound all of it with my roots and filled it with the sound of my apple tree shaking in the wind. But though I hissed bitter regrets and wished a thousand curses on Nourie, I couldn't break the rose trees. The buds grew sick and dark, but they wouldn't die.

***

The prince found me third.

When the apples grew sweet, he came on a bristled boar with battle carved into its tusks. How prettily those scrimshaws of silent soldiers hung above me, scale-armored men casting themselves into death for another man's pleasure. They stood like pillars among my damp and heady breath, those two graceful knaves. They glistened with condensation and sweated me out.

How loftily the boar held its head, so it might not look at anything beneath its opalescent tusks.

He came looking for monsters, with his sword drawn and the hilt well-worn with his hand. He heaved and hawed at the wet bank, cutting down dead trees and blackeyed-susans. The Garden had been abandoned for years and the roses left were a deep and terrible red. My children ran freely through it and left the mark of their claws upon the ground and the dying bark.

"Traveler," I called, so that he started and hewed an apple tree in half, "what news of the Queen of Nightshade and Hemlock?"

He looked about him, gripping the sword as he sweated. His boar snuffled through the grass until it found my corpse, buried under leaves and the rot of apples. The prince didn't lower his sword when his beast cleared the muck from what remained of my face and severed chest, split skin grown about the apple trunk.

"It's said she ate her mother whole," he said. "The King found her cackling in her room, smeared from lip to knee in blood. When she saw him, she only smiled wider and said she'd learned a few poisons of her own. She planted a new garden of bloodroot and foxglove under the Harvest Moon. There's rumors now about her sister, who was said to have died many years ago from tripping into the river."

My bones rattled and ground against each other, but I smiled too. "Do they call her monster yet?"

"It's certainly you who are the monster."

"And you are certainly a prince. What have you to do but kill monsters and kiss princesses? I think you cannot kill me, so I must be a princess and you must kiss me. Come, sir knight of the battle-carved boar. Kiss my lips and see if I awaken. Take me home and lay me in your bed. I'm no virgin and my children may eat you whole, but I am white as snow, black as a crow's wing, and red as blood. There's enough blood in me left that I might spit the rest of me upon you and perhaps your eyes will burn and your tongue fall out. And if you run, I will spit after your heels for severing my trees and tie a witch's curse about your ankles."

"If you are a princess, you can be no monster with curses on her tongue." He looked at me as if I might really be an apple-princess, hidden under some easily broken spell.

I grinned in return. "Has no princess ever screamed and sobbed from her heart and been called whore and witch? Has she never wandered in a garden and called so the trees shook and the servants trembled? Has none ever showed you her tongue to prove she can speak more than the garbled language of ghouls? I am the wailing beast and the mother of monsters and I grow my own poison." I rasped and swelled, so my belly-tree shook and the apples fell down upon the prince and his boar.

When he picked up his sword, my children came crashing through the mint and yarrow. They chattered after him and perhaps they tore him down into the water and drowned him while he bled red as me.

"Monster," they said when they returned. "Monster." They said it giddily, clapping their hands and stumbling into each other. "Monster, monster."

The apples shriveled with winter, grey and streaked in yellow and black. Seeds fell into my mouth and I cracked them between my teeth, gushing poison. The apple stems broke and apples landed in my skeletal fingers, between my thighs, and into my apple-rot cavity.

***

I saw once a pale and ghostly remnant walking on the shore. It came at twilight, along the lavender reflection of the water, trailing a midnight skin of toxin.

Nourie was old by then, with wispy hair and wrinkled hands.

She came slowly, looking under every apple tree and kneeling on arthritic knees to search among the grass and dandelions. At my tree, she dug blind, for the moon was behind the clouds, until the dirt was swept from my skeleton, heady with the scent of apples and fish.

"The monsters have gone quiet," she said, her voice dry and rich, her fingers searching the shape of my skull. "They've left the sheep, and the goats wander in the fields again. But they say Mother – or whoever it is -- lives here now. She's dead now, isn't she? I've seen little of the world the last decade. Does anyone live here beside you? Well, they say her orchard's gone to rot. They say the apples are too poisonous to eat." She grinned up at my apples. "They said I ate her, and you too. They would say such things about us, wouldn't they? As if they never thought about eating their sister's hearts." She opened her hands and set down the finger bone she'd taken so long ago. It gleamed white beside me, well-polished and neatly kept. "I didn't cry or wear black. Mother told me not to. It was much better to smile at them until they tore at their own eyes."

She put her forehead to my skull and her finger in my eye socket. "When I heard how the Garden was dying, I called into the night and hoped you would hear me. Did you? I never could howl like you. And now I'm too old to cast poison petals across bedsheets. I can't even kill a man with a kiss anymore." Her voice went low. "Can I lie beside you? Can I tie my veins to your ribs and grow roots into the rose trees?" She looked up at the roses, still refusing to die, and held me tight. "We should have done it when we were alive. But I can do it now. Your heart blood is still in my belly and if it bursts, it will run over your bones."

She clutched my ribs, apple rot encasing her hand. "Let me turn the roses black as ink until they bleed with my blood."

I couldn't answer. I had no lips. My toe bones clattered and I remembered how I had fallen, how the river had torn through me. I remember how no one punished her and she thought still to come back for my heart. She was the reason I destroyed the trees and learned how to cry.

I wanted to tell her that while she smiled at princes, I disobeyed Mother and cried as hard as Nourie once had. My body rotted and I screamed until I learned how to murder the trees and brew poison. But there'd been no one to speak to. I'd wanted to lay my head into the crook of someone's chin and collar. But there wasn't even an arrogant prince to fall into. My children only touched to tear and break.

I felt the Garden that I had stretched my fingers and knees into, the pulsing rose trees and sour apples, the crabapple tree where the fruit fell and rotted into grass-grown skulls. I ached to know how it would feel to wind myself with another body and burst together through the rose petals.

She lay down beside me and pushed her hands deeper into my ribs. The glut of apple skins stained her sleeves and we lay beneath the Milk Moon.

In the morning, apple blossoms fell into her hair and mouth. She shivered and the wind hummed against her teeth. My roots cradled her as she died, though I wrenched them away when they would have grown into her eyes and around her toes. When the autumn leaves were come and gone, the apples fell between her elbows and knees, caught in the crevices of her body.

The resistance in me broke with her skin. As the ice froze the dead leaves, I ran with blood again. My long-devoured heart-blood spilled from her stomach and stained my ribs. It poured past my teeth and I bound my roots through my sister's breast, her veins kissing my bones. When the trees bloomed again with summer, the trees wilted and the roses bled above us.

Tell Me Something Good

Nicole Lungerhausen

Jenn was knee-deep in a first-trimester-puking-in-between-conference-calls funk. A flat, parched grass veneer lay over her skin, and her boobs remained, much to our mutual disappointment, the same size as they'd been pre-pregnancy. A heat wave the weather app predicted would last five days had stretched to a sticky, interminable ten. My wife needed cheering up and I made it my aim to come to the rescue.

"Oh my God," Jenn said as she unwrapped the box of Dream Awake I'd picked up at the CVS, along with doctor-prescribed pre-natal vitamins and wife-mandated peanut butter cups. We sat at the kitchen table, the coolest room in the apartment, fanning ourselves with fold-out paper fans from Chinatown and sucking on ice cubes. By day six of the heat wave, we'd run through our A/C credits for the month. "Dream Awake. I haven't done this in forever." She cradled the palm-sized, lilac-colored box between her hands. "Have you ever done it?"

"No, never," I said. Jenn flashed me a bright but brief smile. Hard to tell if she really liked the gift or was tamping down a wave of nausea. A feeble breeze wafted through the open kitchen window, bringing intermittent relief from the heat along with the somnolent sounds of reggae from the apartment complex across from ours.

"Duh," she yawned and fanned the back of her neck. "Of course you wouldn't have. This weather is making me a dumbass." She set the box of Dream Awake aside, leaned across the kitchen table and kissed me. "Thank you, baby. This is super sweet of you." Opening her laptop, she zeroed back in on whatever legal document she needed to polish to advance the corporate kleptocratic causes of Burris, Burwell, and Black's clients.

"I thought it'd be fun to do it together, experience what our expanded family will be like." I glanced at the front of the box, which featured a woman with long dark hair gazing blissfully at a vision somewhere in the distance, beyond the borders of the box. I was embarrassed for her, this generically attractive white woman caught up in some marketing exec's cheesy notion of how a person looks while caught up in a daydream. At the same time, I envied how her face radiated with certainty and purpose. How did it feel to see exactly what you wanted in your life, right in front of you?

"Absolutely," Jenn gave my hand a brief squeeze, then she dry swallowed a pre-natal vitamin and followed that up by chomping down a peanut butter cup chaser. Her gaze and fingers drifted back to her laptop. "Later this week, ok?" She pushed the box further towards the edge of the kitchen table. "Gotta finish this brief tonight or my ass is grass."

* * *

We met my first week at the Soap n' Sudz on Telegraph. This tall, fleshy girl in a pink sweatshirt, Cal baseball cap and cut-off jean shorts staggered in under a small bedsheet mountain. I watched her stuff sheets into a series of econo-wall washers, and admired how she stretched and contorted her upper body to get all that cotton-poly blend into each machine. I liked the

no-nonsense way she thrust the coins into the slots on the washers. As her wash spun in soapy circles she dozed, her cap pulled
low across her face. When other people's dryers buzzed, she'd
twitch awake, wipe the side of her mouth and yawn like a kitten.

The water recycler on one of her washers broke and while I took
way more time than necessary to fix it, we got to talking. Jenn was
wrapping up law school at Cal and about to take the bar. Several
classmates were studying and crashing at her place, hence all the
bedsheets. I recited a curated and well-rehearsed list of basics:
new to town, working at the laundromat until I got settled. Her
face lit up when I told her I was an auto mechanic by trade.

"I don't care what you say," she remarked later as we lay tangled
together on the floor of the hive room I rented in a downtown
Oakland sky-rise. Rain drops tapped weakly against the one slim
window. "The best muscle car of 1970 is the Ford Mustang Boss
302, hands down."

"You're pretty sure of yourself." My head rested on the soft pil-
lowed curve of her bare waist, which allowed me to feel and hear
every stomach gurgle, every rumbling laugh. Like most people
who grow up with enough – enough money, enough love, enough
security – Jenn laughed loudly, freely, and often. I was already
100% smitten.

"I am. I absolutely am." She stretched her arms over her head
and accidentally rapped her hands against a storage cubby. She
winced, laughed, and launched into her ten-year plan for her law
career while I kissed her knuckles. "I also want a family," she said
and then elaborated. Two kids, a boy and a girl, with a two and
a half year age gap to maximize sibling closeness while minimiz-
ing negative professional impact on her. Named partner by year
seven. A mid-century modern house with a deck overlooking the

redwoods in the Hills by year nine. "If they're not completely flooded by then." She yawned and gave me a sleepy smile.

"Is that all?" I pulled myself upwards along her torso and let my fingers run along her collarbone. "This can be a one-time thing, you know."

She drew my face close to hers. "I'm not telling you all this to scare you off. I'm telling you this because I like you and I want you to know what I want from my life." She tugged gently on my earlobe. "What do you want, Naomi?"

The question startled me. No one had ever asked me that. In my experience, wants were formless, murky things that drifted below the surface of my consciousness. As soon as they started to float up and take shape, I was made to understand that my wants fell into the category of the nonsensical or the unnatural, sometimes both at once. I didn't know what to say and my heart started to race so I did a dumb thing.

I told Jenn the non-edited version of all my personal history. Coming out to my very God-fearing, very evangelical parentals and three failed run-ins with conversion therapy. Being homeless, first in Modesto and then Lodi, and how I picked up useful survival skills along the way, like stealing and stripping Honda Accords for profit. My recent three-year, two-month stay as a guest of the Central California Women's Correctional Facility.

"Well that's that," I said to no one but myself and the four mildew-colored walls, after Jenn repackaged her abundant curves back into her clothing and departed my hive room, post haste. I'd acted nonchalantly cool in offering my number and she'd done a fairly convincing job of pretending to put it in her phone. I tried to distract myself from disappointment by fixing the loose hinge on the cubby where I stored my meager wardrobe of secondhand jeans and tees and dollar store crew socks. But it was no good. The room still stank of smittenhood cut short and the ghosts of microwaved breakfast burritos past.

Ninety-two minutes later, as a thin, butter-colored bar of light from my one window traveled up the walls of my room, my phone pinged. *Fuck the past. Not supposed to rain today. Walk across the bridge later on and grab some ramen?*

Six months after that, me and Jenn got married and I was pouring french press each morning for my lady love in a kitchen with a real, working four-burner stove, a first for me in a very, very long time.

* * *

"This is amazing," Jenn cradled her phone between her hands, "our baby, in the flesh." She tilted her head and brought the phone closer to her eyes. "Well, in the pixels. But still!" She squeezed my hand and continued to stare at the ultrasound pic. Our eastbound BART train whooshed into the Transbay Tube with a pressurized thunk and metallic whine. I wondered briefly, as I did most times when riding the train under the Bay, if today would be the day plate tectonics would decide to put the tube's underwater construction to the test. I looked over my wife's shoulder and wished I was as thrilled as Jenn about the grainy 3D pic of the 18-week old fetus residing in her womb.

It's not that I wasn't ready to become a parent. I had new gainful employment as a mechanic at Sunny's, an auto shop in Rockridge owned by two Korean brothers who, at the interview, took one look at me and decided to forego a background check. I had a wife eager to be the main incubator for the pair of little Park-Wachsmans we wanted to bring into the world. Plus with all the ass-kicking Jenn was doing at work, it was only a matter of time before our little family moved up even more in the world. It was the right time to get the show on the road.

For the life of me, though, I couldn't picture myself as a parent. Whenever I tried to conjure up mental images of me, Jenn, and the baby together, or even just the baby herself, I drew a total blank. A band of pressure would wrap and tighten itself around my chest. Tackling a tough repair at the shop or skulking around our apartment to suss out broken things to fix were the only ways I could breathe easy again.

"Hey, how about we do the Dream Awake tonight?" Since the night I'd brought the Dream Awake home, Jenn had shifted the box to various places around our apartment, from kitchen table to countertop to the catch-all bin next to the front door. No matter where it landed, the box remained unopened.

Jenn's shoulders tensed and she shifted in her seat. "I don't understand why you keep going on about that stuff. You're getting weirdly obsessive about it."

"I'm not obsessive. I want to experience our future family life in all its living color, 3D glory. And I want to do that with you."

Jenn shrugged. "I know you were enjoying the hospitality of our state's correctional system when it first came out a few years ago but Dream Awake is...I dunno. It isn't anything special. I only did it because it was in the news and all my friends were doing it and I wanted to see what all the fuss was. The experience didn't do anything for me. Honestly, all I remember is feeling a little sick to my stomach afterwards." She smiled. "But that might've been all the Jager I was drinking at the time."

The train ascended from the Transbay Tube and into East Oakland's late afternoon haze with a rush that made my ears pop. "Give it a second chance." I tugged gently on her earlobe and she leaned the side of her head against my palm. "Aren't you curious to see what it will be like? And do that together?"

Jenn's fingers played with the edges of her phone. "Naomi, we don't need some cheap VR nano tech to imagine our family." She tapped the baby ultrasound pic. "We've got all we need right here."

Although she spoke lightly, the corner of her mouth uplifted, there was a "I consider this subject closed" hardness underneath my wife's words that hollowed out my stomach. I didn't want to argue or sink so low as to play the "If you really loved me" card, so I kissed her and said, "Ok, then – tell me something good."

As the skeletal, half-submerged remains of the East Bay's abandoned shipyards whirled past, Jenn leaned her shoulder into mine and described our future family life: organic cloth diapers, work-from-home days, carshare visits to New Pacific Grove. I listened closely, trying to absorb all the details and ignore the band of pressure squeezing my chest.

***

I ended up doing Dream Awake alone.

Now well past the puking stage, Jenn loved to point out the many upsides of being pregnant. "At first I thought of it only as a means to an end," she said as we spent a sweltering Sunday afternoon trawling big-box stores in Dublin for a crib and assorted other baby paraphernalia, "but being pregnant feels sooooo good!" She placed one hand on the six-month baby bump that stretched the confines of her tight black sweater and gestured to her breasts with the other. "Look at my boobs – they're huge! Finally!"

"Finally!" I said with more enthusiasm than I felt. Jeans had been a bad choice for a day-long trip to hot and unlovely exurban Dublin. The dark, thick fabric kept sticking to my legs and the store's instrumental version of "Itsy Bitsy Spider" made my crabbiness and discomfort a hundred times worse.

She bumped my hip with hers and threw a fair-trade wooden teething ring into the cart. "I never have to wait in line for the bathroom and I love how much more space I can take up."

"Hard to imagine taking up space has ever been much of an issue for you."

She cheerfully gave me the finger, then held up a bright orange onesie that read, *just did 9 months on the inside.* "What do you think? Too much?"

"Ha ha. You're hilarious." I took one hand off our shopping cart and rubbed my temples. "Any chance we can get out of here sooner rather than later, baby? The aroma of baby powder-scented everything is making my face hurt."

As my wife's belly swelled, so too did my anxiety. A stubborn and impenetrable blank still lay between me and any visions of my future role as a parent. Once Jenn reached the point of no return in finding a comfortable sleeping position, she said I must be having sympathy insomnia, given the number of times she'd rolled over to find me wide awake. The band that wrapped itself around my chest and slowly squeezed during stressful moments felt as if it'd widened from a thin nylon rope to a hardy canvas strap. Keeping my hands busy fixing one problem or another at the shop or at home no longer provided soothing relief.

No matter how many times I made Jenn paint a happy word picture of our family life, the details didn't stick in my brain, much to my wife's growing annoyance. Cheap VR nano tech seemed to be the only means to an end I needed to see for myself. If I did the Dream Awake, everything would be alright. No, more than alright – it'd be perfect.

So the morning after me and Jenn's baby prep shopping extravaganza, I called in sick to Sunny's Auto. Standing in our kitchen with the open Dream Awake box, I pored over the directions with the care of someone trying to memorize sacred text. I spread some of the Dream Awake nanites, which looked like grains of iron-colored sand, across my palm. They thrummed against my skin like race horses ready to be let out of the starting gate. I breathed out a slow exhale and tipped the nanites in my hand, along with the ones remaining in the box, into a glass filled to the brim with flat ginger ale I'd unearthed from the back of the fridge. I quickly drank the whole glass down, wincing at the metallic aftertaste. After glancing at Jenn's latest ultrasound and my phone's wallpaper, which was a shot of me and Jenn at a friend's wedding, I picked up the directions and recited the activation code.

Within moments, a circle the size of a basketball appeared and hovered at eye level. It had a blue-green shimmer and the light danced up and along the kitchen walls. It reminded me of the water surface of a lighted outdoor pool at night. The light circle continued to expand until it surrounded me and the kitchen disappeared from view. A sense of calm washed over me, followed by a reassuring pressure. It was as if my whole body was being cradled in the palm of a warm, strong hand. My heart throbbed slow and steady in my ears as shapes began to emerge from the shimmering light and resolve. I stepped forward, excited to see the family scene the nanites were sure to root out from my unconscious mind.

What appeared instead was my cell at California Women's

Correctional. Much as I'd left it in real life only...neater, brighter, less antiseptic. A distinct lack of dried-out cockroach corpses and contraband food smells. In place of a scratchy prison blanket the color of fruit mold, an orange and purple batik-style bedspread–identical to the one in my old bedroom at my parent's house in Modesto – lay neatly folded along the metal bar at the foot of the twin bed. Another big difference was the window adjacent to my bunk. It had no glass and sunlight brightened the floor in a rectangular, happy slab.

Pinpricks of light flashed before my eyes and I tried to deepen my shallow breaths. This wasn't what was supposed to happen. Was there something wrong with the Dream Awake? Or was something wrong with me? I tried to recall my deactivation code but no luck. The last remnants of calm vanished and my breath sped up and I thought, "You need to calm the fuck down, Naomi." Disassembled parts for an original alternator for a 1968 Mustang appeared on the bed. I picked up the pulley. The weight of it in my hand, the way its cold metal absorbed the warmth from my palm made me slide into fix-it mode. By the time I put the alternator back together, my breathing had slowed but my insides prickled with residual antsiness. A tidy pile of Car and Driver magazines materialized at the foot of the bunk. Old issues, like the ones I used to thumb through as a kid when my family went to the Turlock Flea Market. I sat down on the bunk and read all the issues, cover to cover.

Later that night in bed, somewhere between reaching to turn off the bedside light and Jenn asking me to rub her lower back, I drifted into an easy and sound sleep.

***

When I walked into the diner in Tracy, he was in a corner booth, the one I'd started to think of as "our booth." I didn't want to be too soft with him, though, so I said, "You're on time, for once."

"Hello to you, too." He smiled and the realness and warmth there surprised me. Of course, odds were 9 in 10 it was the upcoming birth of his first grandkid rather than the sight of his daughter that made him seem genuinely glad to see me.

I nodded towards the empty space on his side of the booth. "I thought you said Mom was coming this time."

He shrugged and made a "what can you do?" gesture. "Your Mom is a woman with strong beliefs. Maybe after the baby is born..." he stared into his coffee cup.

"What? She'll deign to text me back after I send her some cute newborn pics? If I'm lucky? Can hardly wait."

He sighed. "Naomi, I'm trying. I really am."

His face had a gray pallor and his eyes looked pinched at the corners and I needed coffee so I decided to believe him. I slid into the booth, shrugged off my jacket and we launched into a variation of the patter we'd developed since I'd first messaged him six months ago about Jenn's pregnancy. I told him about the mice family I'd found nested in a Tesla's air filter; he told me about the time a customer ended up with a steel-coil mattress wrapped around the entire drive shaft of their Ford F-150. He tried to share his scrambled eggs, bacon, double order of cinnamon raisin English muffins with me; I declined and ordered black coffee and dry toast from the auto kiosk. He commented on how tired I looked, that with the baby I'd need my energy now more than ever; I reminded him that I'd been meeting my own food, shelter, and security needs for some time now, but thanks for the concern. He winced and looked out the window; I apologized by offering up a photo of Jenn's latest ultrasound.

"Can I ask you something?" I said, once he'd ooh-ed and ahh-ed over the ultrasound pic, labeled "30 weeks", on my phone.

"You just did."

"Ha ha." I paused. My index finger tapped out a rapid rhythm against the phone screen. "When Mom was pregnant with me, could you see yourself as a parent?"

At this point, I was staying late at Sunny's so I could do Dream Awake every day. I had yet to see, hear, touch my new family life – my old prison cell always materialized–but I told myself I just needed to keep at it. Plus, more and more doing Dream Awake was the only way I could relax and unwind. Unlike my real life, which was increasingly dominated by "All Things Baby", I could change my environment however I wanted, do whatever I wanted. Wrap the batik bedspread around my shoulders and thumb through old car part catalogs. Daydream about the restoration of the '70 Chevy Chevelle I'd buy someday. Paint the cell's cinder block walls bright blue. Any feeling of ease evaporated the minute I walked in the door at home, and came face-to-face with one or more needs of my immediate future reality. Jenn asking me when I'd be getting around to painting the baby's room. The many sharp and breakable knickknacks scattered throughout the apartment that needed a new home. Even Jenn pressing my palm to her belly and murmuring in my ear "Do you feel that?" sent my heart racing. What made the time spent at home at all bearable was knowing that only a few hours stood between me and my next Dream Awake experience.

"You always asked such odd questions." He chuckled and leaned back against the booth, hands stretched along the top of the pale brown plastic "Of course I saw myself as a parent."

"Could you, like, picture being a dad right away? Or did you start to see it over time?"

"I don't know what you mean. Your mom was pregnant, I was going to be a father. There wasn't any need to picture it. We knew what was going to happen next in our lives."

I sighed, dragged my hand through my hair. "That's not what I'm – did you have daydreams about me?"

His mouth scrunched up as if he'd bitten into something unsavory. "Daydreams? What kind of daydreams?"

"Going to Modesto Baptist on Sundays, riding out to the flea market in Turlock to look for vintage auto parts. Mom doing the books at the shop while you showed me how to change the oil in a car." He stared at me. "You know...daydreams about being together as a family."

He threw me a guarded look, picked up an English muffin half. "I didn't imagine you would turn out as you did, that's for sure."

Past experience told me not to tread further into these familiar but dangerous waters, but I pressed ahead anyway. "Please, I know it's weird, what I'm asking, but I...I can't picture myself as a parent, can't picture the kid. Jenn sees everything so clearly and I can't seem to see us all together, no matter how hard I focus on it–"

He put the muffin half back on the plate. "Naomi, God has given you the chance at a fresh start." He reached across the table, put his hand on mine. "Even with your poor life choices, He still said, 'I choose this lost one to shepherd new life into the world.'

You are so fortunate, so blessed." He let my hand go, scooped up eggs with his fork. "That's real. That's what you should embrace instead of focusing on nonsense like daydreams."

It was as if I was back in my old bedroom in Modesto, Mom and Dad staring at me while I stared back and tried to find words for thoughts and feelings I was struggling to fully understand and square with myself. So familiar, the awful feeling of being scrutinized and found to be both an unfathomable mystery and a heartbreaking disappointment. All the will to be understood went out of me with a great whoosh, like air from a blown tire.

I didn't wait for him to finish breakfast. Made up an excuse about needing to get back to Sunny's because the shop was super busy blah blah blah. He responded with the quick, tight smile of the perpetually disappointed parent. I didn't care if I was letting him down for the hundred thousandth time, and I didn't bother to answer his question about Jenn's due date. By the time I paid the bill and hopped back into the car I'd borrowed from Sunny's, my thoughts were focused on calculating the number of minutes standing between me and my next Dream Awake experience.

***

"Baby?" Jenn stood in the middle of my prison bunk, legs bisected at the knees by the twin bed. She wore a puzzled expression, low-slung jeans, and an "I'm eating tacos for two" t-shirt. A silvery-white crescent of pregnant belly dominated the space where the t-shirt hem ended and the top of her jeans began.

I stared at my wife. Was she part of the Dream Awake experience? The wrench slipped from my fingers. I fumbled to catch it and the confused look on Jenn's face deepened. Nope, definitely not a VR wife, she was the real deal, this woman staring at me as I scrambled to catch a tool only I could see. For a wild half-moment,

I considered making an escape through the open window in my prison cell. But common sense prevailed and I recited my Dream Awake deactivation code. The reality of Sunny's Auto filtered back in, a section at a time. The oil-stained concrete shop floor replaced the batik bedspread packed with transmission parts. The untidy used tire pyramid reappeared in the corner. Jenn stood before me, confused expression unchanged but body no longer bisected by the Dream Awake setting. A blue-striped cloth bag hung from her wrist. The sharp scent of ginger, garlic, and vinegar made my mouth water.

"What are you doing?" she said.

"Nothing." I snatched the empty Dream Awake box from the shop floor and tossed it into the nearest trash bin. "What's up? What are you doing here?" My tone sailed way past the air of breezy nonchalance I was going for and well into the territory of guilty annoyance.

Jenn blinked and tucked her hair behind her ear. "Well, um... you know that big case I've been working on, the one with that sad little organic soap company in Marin suing my client for patent infringement? I got them to reach a settlement. So the partners said, go out, have a good time, celebrate! I thought, I'll drop by Sunny's, surprise Naomi with kimchi stew from that food truck she likes." She raised her hand in a half-hearted wave. "So...surprise."

"Oh."

"You look real happy to see me."

I shook my head. "I'm just...surprised." I forced my mouth upwards into a smile. "See? Yay. Mission accomplished."

"Uh huh." Jenn took a step towards me. She gave me a sly grin, raised her eyebrows. "Were you doing Dream Awake?"

I avoided her gaze. "No. I was...picking up some nuts and bolts from a repair I just finished." I swallowed hard and my stomach rolled. Nothing like the lemony, bitter aftertaste of a lie told badly.

A huff of disbelief escaped Jenn's lips and her gaze slid from me to the rest of the shop, which was devoid of cars up floor jacks, the loud chatter and mutterings of mechanics leaning over open car hoods, the whirring, clanking, and pinging sounds of broken things being taken apart and put back together again. "You said you were working late tonight."

"I am. Well, I was. Like I said, I was just finishing up." Lie #2. My stomach did another somersault. "It's super sweet of you to stop by," I gestured toward the shop sign declaring the presence of chemicals that could harm pregnant women and children, "but you shouldn't be in here, baby." I gently took her elbow and steered her across the shop floor and into the customer waiting room. "You wait here while I finish up and then we'll carshare home, ok?"

Jenn rubbed her lower back, a distracted grimace playing across her face. Then she refocused on me with one of her lemur-clutching-a-branch stares. "No. Not until you tell me what you saw when you did the Dream Awake."

"Baby, I told you, I was just finishing up work–"

An impatient sound rumbled in her throat. She put the bag of take out on one of the waiting room chairs, sat down in another. Taking a deep breath, she sat back with her hands on her belly. "I'm not mad."

"That's funny because you seem pretty mad."

"Ok, I'm a little mad. Not about you doing the Dream Awake. I'm not into it, but if you want to do it, that's your choice." She waved her hand dismissively, as if my choice was an annoying but small bird making a racket outside her window. "It's that you lied about it, just now. It's like you think you did something wrong and now you're trying to hide it from me."

"I'm not trying to hide anything, Jenn." I sounded like the whiny, wayward teen to her older, wiser adult. But her whole attitude – disappointment buoyed by a hearty undercurrent of contempt – got under my skin.

"Great!" She leaned forward, flung her hands out wide. "Then tell me what you saw. I've been telling you all these months what I imagine our kid will look like, what our family will be like. Now it's your turn to share something good with me. I mean, that's the whole reason you wanted to do the Dream Awake in the first place, right?"

"I – I can't."

"Why not?"

"Because it has nothing to do with you or the baby, ok?" The words broke free from my mouth in a sudden burst, then gained speed. "Every time I do Dream Awake, what I see is for me and me alone. Just because this whole situation is happening," I waved my hand toward Jenn's pregnant belly, "doesn't mean you have claim to my entire fucking life."

The ferocity in my voice surprised me. Jenn's head jerked back as if I'd slapped her. She sat down heavily in one of the waiting room chairs, looked up at the ceiling. It felt like forever before she tipped her gaze back towards mine. And when she did there was an unsettled look in her eyes, as if she was seeing something new in me that she hadn't at all expected and didn't care for in the least. "So...it wasn't a one-time thing then. How many times?"

"What?"

"You said, 'every time I do Dream Awake.' Implying that you've done it more than once. How many times?"

I said nothing.

"Wow. You won't even tell me that much? Really?" The disbelief in Jenn's voice made me wince. "Is this because I wouldn't do the Dream Awake with you? Is this some weird passive aggressive revenge thing?" My wife's voice wavered. Her shoulders sagged, deflated of their usual upright confidence. Which was entirely my stupid, thoughtless fault. Heat swept across my face and my anger melted away, replaced by a raw sense of shame.

"No, baby–" I reached for her hand but she stepped back.

"Then what is going on with you, Naomi?" Jenn's eyes jumped around my face and one hand rubbed back and forth across her stomach. "Because I don't know what to think. All I can do is... wonder. Like, I'm wondering if you've been lying to me about working late these past weeks, so you could sit around in your own personal VR bubble doing who knows what. And if you're lying about that, I wonder if you're lying about other stuff, like wanting a family." She put her hands on her knees. "When I saw you sitting on the shop floor, you looked really happy. Like, happier than I've seen you in months. If what's making you happy isn't me and it isn't the baby, then..." She paused. "I don't want to claim all of you, Naomi. But I can't – I won't – be kept at arm's length by you either." She looked away, brushed the corners of her eyes with her fingers.

"I was rebuilding a transmission," I looked her in the eye and my voice came out at a low, steady throttle. "When you came in, that's what was going on. I was in my old cell at California Correctional. That's what happens when I do Dream Awake. I hang out in my old cell and...read car magazines and catalogs, rebuild engine parts for vintage cars. Whatever I want to do, really."

"Oh." She made a noise in her throat that sounded like a cross between a relieved sigh and a strangled laugh. "What kind of transmission was it?

"For a '70 Chevelle. Best muscle car of the year."

A smile, small and sad, flitted across her lips. "Bullshit. The Boss 350 is way better." She glanced out the waiting room window, as a car with a bad muffler gunned it down the street. "My due date's in two weeks."

"Yeah."

"Do you want kids? Do you want to be with me? Do you know what you want at all?"

Jenn had asked me what I wanted once before, back at the beginning, as we lay together in my hive room with the mildew-colored walls. I could tell myself it was my deep love for Jenn that made me adopt her wants and dreams as my own. But I was no selfless romantic. No, the simple, pathetic truth was that I was afraid. Of putting a name to my own wants and dreams. Of shaping my life around them and still ending up with the short end of the stick. Maybe that's why all I could see when I did Dream Awake was my old life. A 4 x 9 foot cell at California Women's Correctional wasn't what I wanted for my future. But at least it was what I knew.

"I'll stop doing Dream Awake. I'll step up. I'll be there for you, I promise." My words came out in a rush, the verbal equivalent of a capsized non-swimmer flailing in deep water for something, anything solid to hold on to.

Jenn wasn't having my panicked half-promises. "I love you. So much. But you need to figure your shit out, Naomi." There was a tenderness to her voice, but she wouldn't look me in the eye. Then she ordered a carshare and left.

***

Yesterday's Dream Awake experience showed me something new.

I'd finished rebuilding the Chevelle transmission and was sitting cross-legged on the bed, staring at the finished product and wondering why I didn't feel more satisfied with it. Thought of taking on another rebuild project – electronic control module maybe?– but quickly pushed the idea away. Restless, I got to my feet and stood in the rectangular beam of sunlight that stretched along the floor. A couple of Dream Awake sessions ago, I'd widened my cell's window into a doorway – it flooded the space with light and made it feel far larger–but I hadn't bothered to look beyond the door frame. I stood in the doorway, placed my palms on the warm, smooth cinder block. A blurry brightness obscured the details of what lay beyond my cell, as if the scene was set with an overexposed filter. The only thing I could make out was a three-foot wide pathway of the greenest and most pristine stretch of grass I'd ever seen. It extended outward from where I stood until it got swallowed up by the overexposed brightness in the middle distance. I took a couple of steps away from the doorway, but still keeping one hand on the frame. A light breeze tickled my cheeks. Further off, shapeless, shadowy figures bent and flitted in and out of all the brightness. Walking down the path and getting closer to those shadows seemed the thing to do. So that's what I did.

The farther I stepped along the path, the more the surroundings changed. The grass shimmered and lengthened to the tops of my knees. When I brushed the blades of grass with my hands, they curled around and softly squeezed my fingers and then fell away. Sunshine dipped down and moonlight dipped up. The shadows began to resolve into sharper shapes. My breath quickened and the nape of my neck prickled but I picked up my pace on the winding pathway, too curious about what lay ahead to be afraid.

Nora's Potion Jar

Emilee Martell

Emilee Martell grew up on a hobby
farm in rural Wisconsin, where she
absorbed innumerable life lessons from
her land and her cats. She attended St.
Olaf College in Minnesota, earning
degrees in English and Environmental
Studies. After college, she spent a year
of service at a community garden in
Denver, Colorado, and now works back
in Wisconsin with a river conservation
organization. In addition to wildly
varied short stories, she writes science
fiction and fantasy novels about social
justice, a broken multiverse, and queer
people of all stripes.

Nora was making a potion in her favorite potion jar. She had combined two cups of mud, four mashed crab apples, a Twizzler, the shredded petals of three marigolds, several fistfuls of grass, a big ball of dead leaves, and five round rocks--one for every year she'd been alive. Soon, Nora reflected happily, she could add six! Then her potions would be better than ever.

For the final ingredient, she was grinding a nubbin of pink chalk down into dust. Nora's potions always worked, always. In the same way she knew to sleep when she was tired and drink water when she was thirsty, she knew exactly what to add to make the perfect potion. Something in her heart told her what to do.

Today, she was making a potion for the sad cat who had been living in the hedge for the past few days. Her dads had tried feeding it, but it ran away whenever they came outside. Nora had watered the sunflowers outside with a special chocolate-syrup-based truth-telling potion, and they told her that the cat was scared because someone mean had kicked him. He needed a boost of strength and bravery, and Nora would make it for him.

Nora scooped up her pile of pink chalk dust and sprinkled it carefully into her potion, then put on the lid and shook it as hard as she could. When her heart told her to stop, she did, lifting the lid off and peering carefully inside. The potion was a thick greeny-brown; a bubble popped on the surface. *Perfect.*

"Here, kitty kitty," she called towards the hedge. "Tasty potion!"

The cat poked his head out of the bushes and eyed her warily. He was a pitiful sight, mangy and flea-bitten with scabs all over his ears. Nora shook the jar at him.

"Tasty potion! Make you feel better!"

The cat's nose quivered as he sniffed the air. Animals could detect the special qualities of a potion; Nora hoped he liked what he smelled. She poured some potion out on the sidewalk and retreated back a few yards. "Come and get it!"

The cat slunk out of the bushes, glancing around fearfully, and crouched by the potion. Nora watched, beaming, as he lapped up a few mouthfuls.

Then he changed. His dull ochre fur turned rich and lustrous. Black stripes raced across his coat and popped in rings up his tail. Shaggy white sideburns burst from his cheekbones. He grew and grew until he stood taller than Nora, and when he looked down at her, his eyes glowed like amber fire.

Nora grinned up at the tiger and patted him on his broad orange nose.

"There," she said proudly. "No one's gonna kick you now!"

The tiger rumbled his agreement deep in his chest and licked her hand. Then he turned, gave her a last grateful, blazing glance, and leapt over the hedge with one effortless bound. Nora saluted him as he loped away into the cornfields.

"Nora?" her work-from-home dad, Graham, called from inside the house. "Did I just hear thunder? Does it look like rain?"

"No, Dad," Nora yelled back. "It was just a tiger purring!"

"Oh, of course." Both Graham and her work-in-town dad, Drew, took her potion accomplishments in stride. Nora wasn't sure they really understood how her talent worked. "It's supposed to storm later though, so keep an eye out!"

"Okay!"

Nora went to the hose to wash out her potion jar. As she stood musing about what to make next--she was torn between a pine needle brew to give squirrels wings or a dandelion milk smoothie that would bring her little horses to life--a familiar sparrow flitted over the lawn and landed in the lilac bush next to her.

"*Nora!*" the sparrow chirped. "*Drew's gonna get home from work early. Graham is making zucchini noodles for dinner. If you take a nap you'll dream about a blue horse.*"

When she had been much littler--only five and a quarter, not almost six--Nora had made some of the same revitalizing potion she'd used on the cat for a sick sparrow she'd found on the lawn. But she wasn't as talented a potion-maker back then, and she'd used green chalk instead of pink, and instead of turning the sparrow into an eagle like she'd meant to, the potion had given the bird the ability to see the future. It was a little weird, to be honest, but she didn't want to hurt the sparrow's feelings.

"Thanks," she told the bird. "That sounds like it would be a cool dream."

"*Also, Nora!*" the sparrow trilled. "*Lightning will strike your house tonight and burn it down.*"

Nora frowned. That didn't sound good.

"What do you mean, burn it down? Like, the whole thing? With us in it?"

"Lightning will strike your house tonight and burn it down!"

The sparrow was not super articulate. It also had a short attention span, and darted away again before Nora could ask it more. She stood with the hose still running, lost in thought. She didn't want her house to burn down, but would her parents believe her if she told them what the sparrow had said? And could Drew and Graham stop a lightning storm? Her dads were almost invincible, Nora knew, but a storm seemed like it might be too big even for them.

Her heart nudged her. *Potion.*

Nora beamed. Of course! All her worries fell away. She'd make a potion to protect the house, and everything would be just fine.

She skipped her nap, with some regrets over missing the blue-horse dream, and spent the afternoon racing back and forth across the yard. This was the most complicated potion she had ever made. Sand from an anthill, petals from a coneflower, bark from a grape vine, spit from Graham--that one took some cajoling--and a dozen other ingredients, all stirred together with a maple twig and an oak twig and a braided stalk of grass, in that order, clockwise and counter-clockwise and finally flipped upside down and shaken until Nora's arms turned noodly.

Then, following her heart's instructions, she dabbed globs of her potion all around the base of the house, scraping out the very last bits to draw a smiley face on the front door. Then Nora leaned back, exhausted. It was almost time for dinner. She was looking forward to zucchini noodles.

But then she realized that there was still a nudging in her chest. She wasn't done yet.

The last ingredient, her heart told her, was the glass shards of her potion jar.

Nora's lip trembled. She didn't want to smash her potion jar. She didn't know if she could make potions without it, and she loved making potions, more than anything.

Well, almost more than anything. She loved her dads and her house the most.

"Is the bird right?" she asked the truth-telling sunflowers. "Will my house burn down without this?"

They nodded their broad yellow heads. "*Yes, yes.*"

Nora heaved a great sigh. Being a potion-maker, she reflected, was a hard business. "Okay."

She held the jar high above her head, then dropped it on the sidewalk. It shattered with a crack like the world splitting in two.

"Nora!" Graham was outside in a flash. "What happened? Are you all right?"

"I dropped my jar," Nora mumbled, and she couldn't stop two fat tears from dripping down her cheeks.

"Oh, my darling." Graham scooped her up. "We'll get you another one, don't worry!"

"But what if it doesn't work the same?" Nora wailed.

"It isn't the jar that makes your potions special, silly!" Her dad smiled. "It's you!"

Nora sniffled. "Really?"

Graham carried her inside. "Promise."

Drew came home and said the same thing when Nora told him what had happened to her jar. Mostly reassured, Nora ate her dinner--the noodles were very good--and then went to bed, very tired and still a little sad. She tumbled into exhausted sleep just as raindrops started pounding on the roof.

A few hours later, Nora woke to a flash of pure white light in her window and a crack like the world splitting in two. The house shook like a giant had slammed his fist down on it. Downstairs, her dads shouted.

"I think it hit the house!" she heard Drew yell. "I'll go check--"

The front door opened and slammed. Rain slashed across Nora's window.

Graham's footsteps came thumping up the stairs. "Nora--"

"I'm fine!" Nora called. "The house is fine too."

Graham burst into her room. "Nora! You must be so scared--it's going to be okay--"

Nora yawned. "Actually, I'm just pretty tired."

Graham didn't look like he believed her. His face was as frightened as the cat's had been before it was a tiger. *I should make him some potion tomorrow,* Nora reflected sleepily, *to help him be braver, like me.*

Use sugar instead of chalk, her heart whispered, *unless you want him turning into a tiger.*

What about the jar?

Who needs a jar?

The front door opened again. "Never mind, it must have missed us," Drew called. "Not a scratch on the house. Everything's okay!"

Nora settled back into bed and smiled. Her potions always worked. Always.

Slipping Through the Stars

Laura J. Campbell

Laura Campbell lives and writes in
Houston, Texas. She is encouraged
in her craft by her husband, Patrick,
and children, Alexander & Samantha.
Mrs. Campbell won the 2007 James
B. Baker Award for short story for her
science fiction tale, 416175. About three
dozen of her short stories have appeared
in Pressure Suite: Digital Science
Fiction Anthology 3, Under the Full
Moon's Light (Anthology), Well Said,
O Toothless One (Anthology), Liquid
Imagination, Suspense Unimagined,
Gods & Services (Anthology), Page &
Spine, Breath and Shadow, and other
venues. Her two novels, "Blue Team
One" and "Five Houses," are currently
available online.

There weren't many planets that still had royalty. But Sri'Quis was one of the few planets ruled by a male-preference primogeniture monarchy. With her son now in power, Queen Mother Rigel had been ordered to leave the planet and surrender herself to voluntary exile. Her absence was intended to dissuade the ambitions and plots of those who believed that Queen Rigel should still rule. This in turn afforded her son, Torin IX, sufficient assurance that his claim to the throne was uncontested.

The Queen Mother was sitting in an opulent stateroom onboard the Earth-ship *Onyx*, reconciling herself to a future of relative irrelevance. She was dissatisfied with that.

"When will we arrive at Lough Derg?" she asked.

"Soon," her Sri'Quisian bodyguard, Oirin, told her. Oirin was tall and healthy, with strong muscles and silver-colored eyes. His head was shaved a perfect bald; he applied wax to his scalp, making his dome shine.

"They tell me the planet is named after an island on Earth."

"Earth's Lough Derg is an island sanctuary, surrounded by water," Oirin confirmed. "As Lough Derg is a water-covered planet, save for the solitary island that holds your future palace and a few other destinations, the Earthlings chose the name to reflect the similarity to Lough Derg on their home planet."

"Earthlings. We are resorting to the company of *Earthlings*. I once ruled over seventeen planets. People obeyed me. And now I must accept the charity of these newcomers?"

"The Uoy have been stepping up their attacks in our systems," Oirin reminded her, pointing out the mounting aggression of Sri'Quis's and Earth's mutual enemy, the war-loving Uoy. "Earth has had remarkable success in fighting the Uoy. Their territorial planets are quite safe. And this particular planet—Lough Derg—is still close enough to Sri'Quis that you could arrive in a timely manner, should you be called upon to attend to official Sri'Quisian business."

"Torin will not call upon me," Rigel assured her bodyguard. "He has an ambitious wife and he has surrounded himself with newly powerful men and women who do not want me—nor the remnants of my Court—anywhere near them. In their shoes, I would have had me killed. But I suppose that sort of public malfeasance might engender some disregard for Torin. He can afford to alienate himself from my more vocal supporters, but he cannot afford to alienate himself from those factions that are currently pledged neither to him nor me."

"Earth is neutral to Sri'Quisian politics."

"Hardly. They are as embroiled in our internal quarrels as any Sri'Quisian. The Earthlings are using me. By keeping me alive in their pretty little palace-prison they will enjoy enhanced bargaining power with Torin and the Sri'Quis government. Cunning little devils, these Earthlings. The universe was so much simpler before they were introduced among the space-faring."

"The Earthlings have assigned an Earth-born bodyguard to protect you," Oirin added. "A woman named Mary Osprey. She has just been transported to this vessel."

"They can't even make up a convincing false name," Rigel noted. "*Osprey*. A large predatory bird that lives by the water. When we are going to our exile on a water planet. No doubt our new acquaintance has a hidden identity. Perhaps many."

"All you need know is that I will stand resolutely by your side," Oirin assured the displaced queen.

"Nobody has ever stood resolutely by my side. Not even my King and husband. He died, and left me to the mouth-breathers and predators of Sri'Quis. He made no accommodation for my safety. If not for these meddling Earthlings, I would be dead. It was they who saved me, mere moments before the assassination attempt."

"But you are safe now, Majesty," Oirin replied.

"Earthlings," she whispered, listening to the low hum of the *Onyx's* engines. "How I loathe them. Why couldn't *anybody* else have provided my salvation?"

***

"Well, this is awkward," Rigel said upon meeting Mary Osprey. "I was hoping to complain about how ugly you were. But here we are."

The two women bore striking similarity to one another. They were both tall, with reddish-blonde hair that cascaded in waves over their shoulders; their lips were thin, with the corners tending to droop downwards, as if perpetually on the verge of frowning. Their eyes were slightly large, with a subtle almond shape, their noses large and aquiline. They had a faintly bulbous firmness to their chins and broad squared foreheads. Had the exiled former queen of Sri'Quis and her unwanted guardian from Earth claimed to be mother and daughter, nobody would have disputed the claim.

"I am Dr. Mary Osprey," the Earth woman greeted. "Earth Secret Service. I will attend to your safety from this point onward."

"Constant surveillance?" Rigel recognized. Someone on Earth knew her vanity well; they had sent a copy of her own youth to protect her. It engendered a certain level of acceptance from the Sri'Quisian queen. She sensed her desire to hate the young woman already being underwhelmed.

"I am sure that we are both ever constant and certain," Mary replied.

"Walk with me," Rigel said. "I find extended space travel tedious."

"We will be at Lough Derg soon."

"Will I be safe there? There has already been one attempt to take my life. I was told there was another plot against me, designed to assure that I never arrive at Lough Derg alive."

"On board the *Onyx* you are relatively safe," Mary replied. "We are in a controlled environment. Should anything threaten you here, all possible suspects are likely to be on board, either as perpetrators or accessories to any villainy. But once at Lough Derg, people may come and go with much more stealth. You will have to spend your life within the protective walls of the Patrician Palace, which is being prepared for your safe residency. Your ladies-in-waiting have already arrived there and are decorating your apartments, so that all you will need to do when you arrive is walk in and assume occupancy. But bear in mind, it will *always* be dangerous for you outside of those walls."

"There is only one island on that drowned little world? No other land?"

"The island is large enough for your palace, a monastery of our St. Patrick, three good-sized cities, adequate cropland, a large freshwater lake, and a spaceport—with all the luxuries and infamies that generally accompany spaceports."

"My son chose my exile well," Rigel noted. "You know, Torin and I once got along magnificently. But he has allowed his ambition to veto my counsel. We are rivals now." She looked at Mary. "You aren't even asking me about the rumors?"

"Rumors are of questionable intelligence value," Mary stated. "I do not put my trust in the unsubstantiated."

"So, you *have* heard the rumors."

"I was fully briefed for my assignment," Mary replied. "Knowing the Sri'Quisian gossip could give me insight into the motivations of those who might plot to harm you. And keeping you from harm is my job."

"Do you want to know if any of them are true? *The rumors?*"

"It does not matter to my position, if the rumors are true or not. Therefore, I do not need to know if they are true or not. I do not dally in supposition."

"I should have had you as a daughter," Rigel found herself saying. "A level-headed woman who does not wrestle with shadows when she recognizes that there are facts to administer."

Mary started to direct them back to the safety of Rigel's quarters aboard the *Onyx*.

"Back to my cell?" Rigel asked. "It is a cell, by the way. It has an airlock as a door and no windows. What was this area used for before my occupying it, if not a prison cell? There are little cameras that float about the area, capturing images. I am scarcely afforded privacy. My bathroom is the only place I can find any modesty."

"The *Onyx* is a Letter of Marque ship," Mary replied. "They have occasion to take on prisoners. Your quarters are a reconfiguration of the brig. It was remodeled, to provide a reading room for you, a bedroom, a bathroom, a small kitchen, and a living area. The rooms were decorated in attempt to reflect your culture's opulence—and disguise the fact that the rooms occupy the brig's space. But this 'cell' is not to lock you in, but to keep would-be assassins out. Only you, your bodyguard Oirin, the captain of the *Onyx*, and myself have access to the area."

"I was promised that this ship was safe."

"Captain Crowchun and her crew are undeniably safe. But should this vessel be boarded by hostile forces, Uoy mercenaries for example, we wanted you in a secure location. The airlock on your quarters secures *you*. You are safely in Earth custody now. We aim to keep you healthy, alert, and alive."

"You need me healthy, alert, and alive—to employ as a Queen against my son, the King, as if we are pieces of a living version of your Earth game chess. And you do not mince words, I notice. *Custody.* Not even an attempt to hide my status. A queen who is being used as a pawn."

"I don't mince words. And I don't play games."

"Hmmm. You will have to work with my Sri'Quisian bodyguard, Oirin," Rigel noted. "Do not let him go to your head. He has a crude passion for Earth women. He fetishizes them. And he is quite charming."

"I am asexual," Mary answered. "I have no desire for men nor women. My Sri'Quisian counterpart can indulge his crude imagination on his own time. My only focus is on keeping you safe."

"Are all of your corps like you?" Rigel asked.

Mary did not really smile, but her eyebrows rose in contemplation as she answered: "There is *nobody* else like me. So, in that regard, yes—all of my corps are like me."

***

Captain Morgana Crowchun was a woman who emanated energy. She was slightly plump, with wild curly chestnut-colored hair and flashing black eyes. Her skin was nearly white, a trait she enhanced by covering her exposed flesh with heavy white makeup. She indulged in a wardrobe that imitated the privateers of Earth's Queen Elizabeth I's era, dressing herself in rich fabrics embellished with heavy, intricate, gold-threaded embroidery. She even carried an old-fashioned cutlass sword with a gilded handle. She was proficient in its use, spending hours sparring with an android programmed specifically for the task of practicing swordsmanship with Captain Crowchun.

Mary stood at attention. "You wished to update me on our progress?"

"We will be at Lough Derg in three hours. Arguably the most critical phase of your mission. Getting Rigel to Lough Derg alive."

"Do we detect any approaching vessels?"

"No."

"That almost concerns me. Intel stated that Torin wanted his mother to suffer a misadventure before she arrived at Lough Derg."

"Torin claims that his mother—that regal little old lady we have in our redecorated brig—killed his father." Morgana poured them each a glass of red wine. "King Torin IX says he wishes to avenge his father's untimely death. Anyway, that is the story, if you wish to subscribe to gossip. Please, sit. You are my colleague, not my subordinate."

Mary Osprey sat down.

"Should we toast to something?" Morgana asked, raising her glass.

"Why? There is nothing in particular to toast to. We should simply drink. I see no purpose in frivolous gestures."

"Slàinte, then."

They drank. Mary said nothing.

"Rumor, as you no doubt know, reported that King Dorhath was fooling around on Rigel," Crowchun recited. "And that in retaliation for his dalliances, Rigel had him poisoned. So that her philandering husband would no longer vex her and her doting son could assume the throne."

"I have heard the gossip. Do you have anything that substantiates it to the level of intelligence?"

"Dorhath had ordered a shipment of Praven figs, his favorite fruit, from an Earth Herschel Colony planet named Gripinnia. Intel, which cannot reveal its methods nor its sources, confirms that while in transit the fruit shipment was momentarily—and secretly—diverted onto a pirate ship named the *Sea Foam*. After a short detour on board that criminal vessel, the figs were clandestinely placed back in the hold of the original ship, their brief absence undetected, and delivered as promised."

"Sri'Quis sources validate that the figs passed all toxin screens upon delivery, and that others ate from the same batch of figs with no ill effect," Mary reminded her.

"Dorhath mysteriously stopped breathing exactly four hours after consuming those figs." Morgana replied knowingly. "Do you know who is counted among the crew of the *Sea Foam*? I mean, it is a very notorious ship. Earth Navy has been hunting them for years. There is an astounding reward to be paid out to whoever aids in their capture."

"Dr. Ursula Manning, a former Earth Secret Service long-range recon agent, who has turned pirate, serves as physician and chef on board the *Sea Foam*," Mary replied. It was obvious that Morgana already knew that.

"My sources tell me that if Dr. Ursula Manning was protecting somebody, that anyone with ill-intent towards the person in her care would meet a mysterious demise *long* before they ever had the opportunity to harm their target. Manning operates as a pre-emptive strike in the assassination world. And I use the present tense intentionally. Amazing how playing pirate can enable an even more sinister role. What was her code name—*is* her code name? Ah, yes. It was told to me. *Aize'Rcul*. I thought it an odd codename, so I spelled it backwards. And you know what I discovered? *Lucrezia*. As in Lucrezia Borgia, a woman with a reputation for excelling in the fine art of poisoning. They say that if Dr. Ursula Manning is in possession of one single cell from your body, she can concoct any number of poisons designed to paralyze you, alter your perceptions, modulate your inhibitions, affect your memory, make you ill, or even kill you—and *you alone*. And my Intel has Aize'Rcul alone with that consignment of figs for over three hours. I suspect that Earth Secret Service has more than one of their own protecting Earth's latest asset, the Queen Mother Rigel."

"I would not know the full operational strategy of the Service," Mary recited.

"I believe that. You have probably been told only what you need to know. Listen to me, Dr. Osprey: The *Onyx* is a *Marque* vessel, *not a pirate ship*. I operate within the boundaries of my Letter of Marque. My ship engages in *legal* business. And I do not imperil my crew, my ship, or my Letter. There will be no cloak-and-dagger bullshit on board the *Onyx*. Do we understand one another?"

"Of course. Your affinity for low-risk operations is one of the attributes that recommended your ship to us. But, I do have one request, to further enable me to perform my duties. Who knows what we may have already brought aboard?"

"What do you want?"

"I want full access to all data flowing in and out of Rigel's quarters. She farts, I want to smell it."

"You have full brig-quality surveillance already."

"I want *everything*. Temperature, light levels, audio, visual, full logs of who goes in and out and when. Acquiescing to a legal surveillance request from an Earth agency is within the boundaries of your Letter of Marque."

"And therefore you have it," Morgana replied. "As you said, it is within my Letter, and I am being paid by Earth Secret Service for this run. So, for this request, I will indulge my customer. I will deploy whatever additional devices and equipment you need to the area. But you take the data you generate with you.

All of it. I don't want Torin's lackeys showing up and demanding those records."

"What records?" Mary smiled.

"Exactly."

***

Mary Osprey's next briefing was with Oirin. They were on final approach to Lough Derg and it was time to become acquainted and finalize their landing plans.

Oirin smelled wonderful. He had anointed himself with cologne; his shaved hair was perfectly waxed. His silver eyes were radiant. He bowed to Mary with a flourish. "I had heard that you were beautiful," he greeted flamboyantly.

"From who?"

"Pardon?"

"Who told you I was beautiful? Please provide their name."

"It is a greeting," Oirin said, sitting down in a chair with an expression of mock dejection. "Earth women like being complimented on their appearance."

"Appearance is a shallow platform to judge people by. And, not all Earth women indulge in such vanity. Physical appearance is not currency; a person's value is not determined by how much you enjoy looking at them. Additionally, if you did not truly mean what you said, then the statement reflects poorly upon your veracity."

"Well, what should I say, then?"

"I am interested in facts and honesty," Mary replied. "We need to get the Lady Rigel from the *Onyx* to the palace on Lough Derg as quickly as possible. This is the entirety of our conversation."

"We will get her to her palace quickly enough. A parade is planned to celebrate her arrival. There is a small population of Sri'Quisian expats on Lough Derg, as well as members of her court already in residence at the palace. Lady Rigel's supporters on Lough Derg desire to see their Queen. The parade will not take long."

"The parade will not happen."

"What do you mean? *Of course it will happen.* Queen Rigel is a queen, not a prisoner."

"She is a *target*," Mary answered firmly. "And targets do not dally idly in the streets where would-be assassins can take easy aim at them. Lady Rigel will be transported in an armored vehicle, directly from the *Onyx* to the Patrician Palace on Lough Derg. I already have agents sweeping the palace grounds—again—for any dangers."

"Make no mistake, Dr. Osprey, I, also, am pledged to die for my monarch. But you do not know our ways," Oirin replied, equally firmly. "Some fanfare is *required*. She must appear fearless, not fearful. It is bad enough that you have stuffed her in a brig for this journey."

"This vessel provides superior protection," Mary noted. "Captain Crowchun is renowned for her ability to evade attacking vessels. The brig—and yes I acknowledge that it *is* the brig—is a very secure space."

"There are eight people on this ship," Oirin reminded her. "Six Earthlings, the Queen Mother, and myself. I agree with you that Queen Rigel is safe here. That is why she should be walking around at will aboard this vessel, owning it. Not confined to a cell. "

"The parade is a no-go," Mary reiterated. "Rigel can deliver her greetings via a video link, once she is safe inside the palace."

"The parade *will* happen," Oirin replied harshly. "*It is our way.* Our monarchs must be seen by their people."

"How long have you served Rigel?"

"Over ten years," Oirin replied. "I was her guardian while she and Torin spent their summers at the Sand Palace on Sri'Quis. I was there when the assassination attempt was made."

"The one we Earthlings thwarted."

"It was fortuitous for Earth that your agent caught the would-be assassin with the knife in his hand. The attacker had plotted a crude method of execution for our Queen. Very unsophisticated."

"Death has never required technology," Mary said. "Captain Crowchun, for example, is adept with a sword—a bladed weapon. It is just as deadly as any energy-based weapon. The would-be assassin—he was identified as loyal to Torin. He had authored a manifesto, explaining that as long as Rigel lived, she posed a credible threat to Torin's power. And that, therefore, in the assassin's mind, Rigel needed to be out of the way—permanently—in order to preserve peace on Sri'Quis."

"I am familiar with the assassin's motivations. After all, I was there. You were not."

"No parade, no precession, no leisurely stroll," Mary said. "This mission is under Earth governance. We call the shots."

"The shots? As in weapon shots?"

"Actually, yes. No weapon formed against Lady Rigel shall prosper while Earth Secret Service has a say in the matter."

"You think you're some sort of god? To tell a queen what she will do?"

"In the Service we note that God sees even the sparrow as it falls. It is our job is to make sure that the bird never dies to begin with. We do our duty to alleviate God's anguish. Likewise, there shall be no mourning among Rigel's supporters."

She stood up and leaned over the table at Oirin. "Just make sure that we are crystal clear: *there will be no parade.*"

She turned and left, feeling the resentment from Oirin following her.

Perhaps his encounter with her had tarnished his fascination with Earth women.

***

In the old days of the Cold War on Earth, espionage agents would sometimes possess the hotel room beneath a visiting target, performing duties from eavesdropping to gathering human waste from the above-room's sewage line to deduce the medical condition and chemical habits of the target.

Mary Osprey was not a spy, *per se.* She was a protective special agent.

Rigel was correct: there was great value for Earth in keeping Rigel alive. Earth needed Torin unsettled. Sri'Quis was situated next to a space-folding rift that could transport enemy ships very close to Earth in very little time. And Sri'Quis had abundant reserves of the rare metals needed for inter-stellar space-craft construction. Earth, new to space-faring, wanted preferential access to those materials.

Earth wanted Sri'Quis to consider itself indebted to Earth.

Earth also wanted Torin to know that if he disagreed with Earth directives and requests, a powerful rival for his throne could be produced off of Lough Derg in a moment's notice.

Mary watched every possible reading registering the conditions in Rigel's rooms aboard the *Onyx*. That the Queen's quarters had been designed to fit in the brig was helpful; numerous streams of data were already programmed to monitor the self-contained space. A series of mobile cameras were deployed in the brig, capturing images from Rigel's quarters. Only her bathroom was off-limits to the cameras, granting Rigel some privacy.

Mary sat attentively at the monitors. Rigel had adjusted the thermostat to 80 degrees Fahrenheit—Sri'Quisians liked it warm. There was very little humidity, and a perfect one atmosphere of pressure. Rigel had scented the air with lavender, and the lighting was soft and golden.

Rigel was in the bathroom, attending to her personal hygiene. The bathroom was a self-contained space within the brig, fashioned from the brig's solitary confinement cell. It was not a very large space—only ten cubic meters, but it sufficed for this journey.

"One hour to Lough Derg," Morgana Crowchun reported over an intercom. It was an open access announcement.

Rigel exited the bathroom, and allowed herself a regal sigh. Her face seemed to instantly age ten more years, contemplating the imminence of her exile.

"Uneasy lies the head that wears a crown," Mary recited. "Shakespeare's *Henry IV, Part II*. I'll get a copy of *The Complete Works of Shakespeare* for you to read, Rigel. You'll find you have a lot in common with some of his characters. We can discuss his plays. I have two doctorates—one in physics, the other in English Literature. The latter, hopefully, will be the most useful for all of our future conversations."

Rigel loosened her jacket, indicating she was becoming slightly warm. She rubbed her head, as if she was getting the hint of a headache.

Mary consulted the gauges. The statistics for Rigel's quarters were constant, except for one reading: the bathroom, its door closed, now registered slightly less than one atmosphere.

Mary kept her eye on the data. A minute clicked by. The atmospheric pressure inside the bathroom dropped a little more. It was a steady decline.

Mary got up and exited the room.

She activated the entrance to Rigel's quarters. "Accompany me," she commanded.

"What is the meaning of this?" Rigel exclaimed. "Barging in here unannounced? Have you Earthlings no couth?"

"The atmospheric pressure is dropping in your quarters," Mary explained. "I see no cause for the drop. We need to evacuate you, as a precaution."

Rigel was unresponsive.

"I have pledged to take a bullet for you, as my duty," Mary said. "And that duty encompasses pulling your sorry royal ass out of the way of an oncoming bullet if I feel justified to do so."

Rigel was aghast, but now responsive. She sensed Mary's urgency.

"This is not a drill?"

"Majesty," Mary implored. "We need to get out of this room now. If the pressure falls just a little bit more the air locks to these rooms will close this room off, to protect the ship. We will both be trapped in here if we stay. We could both die."

Rigel obediently accompanied Mary.

"Where are we going?" Rigel asked

"My quarters," Mary replied. "Do not alert anyone. Repeat—do not alert *anyone*."

As they reached the door to Mary's adjacent quarters, the heavy air-lock door to the brig slammed shut. Its gears let out a hollow screeching noise as they sealed off the rooms that had served as Rigel's quarters. A series of orange lights began to glow in the hallways.

"We detected a pressure loss in the brig," Morgana reported, using the secure communications line into Mary's quarters. "Rigel?"

"She is safe with me," Mary reported. "I want an Earth guard outside of my room. And do not report anything to anyone. Turn off the orange alarm and tell everybody it was a test of the system. I don't know what is going on yet."

"It must have some logical explanation," Rigel suggested. "I will call on Oirin..."

"Negative," Mary insisted. "You must trust me, Majesty. I need to be in full control of the flow of information right now. Nobody is to know where you are, or how you are, except for the Captain and me."

Rigel nodded. "Since you have started calling me 'Majesty,' I will presume there is some gravitas to your concerns. I will abide by your counsel for now."

***

Rigel was sitting in a chair in Mary's room, apprehensive yet royally composed.

Morgana entered, careful not to let the guard know that he was guarding not only Mary, but Rigel, as well.

"Oirin is being a pain in the ass," Morgana reported. "He keeps asking if Rigel is all right or if her quarters have been compromised. I don't know how much longer I can stall him. We are thirty minutes from Lough Derg. What do you have for me?"

"The bathroom is self-contained—it was fashioned from the solitary confinement cell. It has a volume of ten cubic meters and was being maintained at eighty degrees Fahrenheit and one atmosphere. It took 344 seconds for the pressure to fall to 0.5 atmosphere and the airlock to automatically separate the rooms from the rest of the ship. About six minutes. Utilizing Fliegner's Formula and the equations associated with compressible fluid flow, there must have been a small leak in that room."

"But how?"

Mary used remote commands to open the bathroom door and pilot a remotely controlled mobile camera into the room. She scanned the walls, eventually visualizing a small dark circular aberration. She directed the floating camera closer to the object, located in a corner and partially hidden by a bathroom rug. "There," she pointed. "A one centimeter by one centimeter hole. Crudely rendered in the wall that connects to the outer hull of the *Onyx*. You can see the tool marks on the wall. There is a deposit of chalky residue – suggestive of a metal dissolving chemical being poured into the hole – it took a while to work through the metal and make the hole."

"If you hadn't gotten her out of there, Rigel would be dead," Morgana noted. "The triggered air-lock would have trapped her inside, to safeguard the rest of the ship. The air inside the quarters has evacuated into outer space. There's no way she would have survived."

"Somebody is going to be very unhappy when we land with Rigel alive," Mary noted.

"Thank you for saving my life," Rigel said to Mary, looking at the images from her now segregated quarters. The Queen Mother was expressing both gratitude and embarrassment.

"Who did this? Who endangered my crew and ship?" Morgana asked.

"I will find out, I promise," Mary replied. "The air-lock contained the room. The rest of the ship is safe. You can expect repairs once we are on Lough Derg. I will get Rigel to the Patrician Palace as soon as we land. No fanfare, no parade." "My life is in your debt," Rigel acknowledged. "I will do as you direct."

***

Mary Osprey had Rigel dress in the uniform of female junior officer from the *Onyx's* crew. She ushered the former queen into a plain hovercraft car and they began an unheralded trip towards the palace. The manifest listed that Mary and the putative crewmember of the *Onyx* were traveling ahead to secure the palace grounds.

Oirin was instructed that he would accompany a regal-looking heavily-shielded hovercraft that presumptively carried Rigel inside. He was instructed that there could be no communication with Rigel while she was 'in' the royal transport, owing to security concerns on the ground.

He seemed stressed and confused, but he acquiesced. He really had no other option.

Mary was keenly observant as Rigel and she traveled towards the security of the isolated palace on the isolated island on the isolated planet.

"You never asked me about the rumors," Rigel said, tiring of the silence.

"I told you that I don't need to know."

"I want you to know," Rigel said. "You risked your life coming into that room and rescuing me. The least I can do is let you know everything you need to know."

Mary said nothing.

"I knew that my husband was an adulterer," Rigel said. "I would have had to be an imbecile not to know it. He had private communications, received clandestine messages, and he would appear with new items—gifts from his whore. He would pass the items off as something he had just 'found' or say that they had been given to him by a dignitary for whom there was no record of visiting the palace. He would explain the conversations he *had* to have away from my presence as privileged discussions with his advisors. I overheard him tell his mistress: 'I love you more than anybody else in the galaxies.' Can you imagine how I felt? I ruled our empire while he philandered. The satisfaction of the people, the power of our planet and our protectorate systems—that was all *my* doing. *I* brokered the alliances that brought three new planets into our empire, *I* managed the administration of our government, *I* set up the financial policies that have fueled Sri'Quis to greatest prosperity it has ever seen, and *I* established the social changes that yielded the highest public satisfaction levels in our empire's history. *I* oversaw the increased commerce of our colony planets. *I* built our military forces up so that we could provide a counter-threat to the ever increasing aggression and provocation of the Uoy. *The Uoy—the only planetary people I despise even more than Earthlings.* And, while we are on that subject, it was *I* who managed the détente with Earth. Yet he loved *her* more? It wasn't jealousy, so much as feeling unacknowledged and ridiculed. I detested being made to look like a clown. But I endured it. For decades, I endured it. *I* was the queen. *I* was the wife. I had my own authority, my own legitimacy. I may have *wished* Dorhath dead on occasion, but I never killed him, nor did I ever order him killed. Torin spread that rumor, to discredit me. I lost my husband and my son. Now all I have left is a title and a handful of obligated servants. *You* may be the only honest person I have in my life. An *Earthling*. A *commoner*. I never thought it would come to this."

Mary remained silent. The list of accomplishments that Rigel cited were exactly the reasons Earth wanted her alive and on their side of the board.

"Do you believe me?" Rigel asked.

"It doesn't matter what I believe," Mary replied. "I honor your majesty according to my duty. No more, no less."

Rigel was silent for a moment.

"Thank you, Dr. Osprey," Rigel finally said, her countenance calming. "You provide me with candid respect. I apologize for my rudeness. It is unbecoming of my station. I hope that you can forgive an old woman for a moment of foolishness expressed in a very trying time. It may take me a while to adjust to having an honest person in my life."

* * *

Mary watched the fully repaired *Onyx* as it lifted from the bay in the spaceport, rose into the early morning sky, and disappeared into the crucible of space.

She retreated into her apartments at the Patrician Palace, and logged onto her secured communication lines. Outside her window she could see the vast ocean that surrounded the island.

"Cecil," a female voice greeted. "How is my sister-in-arms today?"

"I am living a bodyguard's life. How are you, Special Agent Aize'Rcul?" Mary replied. It had been a while since she had been addressed by her own codename, *Cecil*. "As you well know, it is a pirate's life for me," Aize'Rcul answered. "I heard there was nearly a misadventure upon the *Onyx*."

"I have a suspect in that misadventure," Mary replied. "But I wished to call upon your special insight, as you seem individually familiar with the royal house of Sri'Quis and its tragedies."

"Tell me your suspicions. I will tell you no lies."

"There were only a few people who had access to Rigel's quarters on board the *Onyx*, much less her bathroom."

"The captain of the *Onyx*, for example," Aize'Rcul noted. "That odd creature, Captain Morgana Crowchun. With her garish white make-up and her habit of dressing herself up like Sir Walter Raleigh."

"Crowchun had opportunity and means to create a hundred scenarios in which Rigel could have been killed, without risking the entire ship. A hole in the hull, with air leaking out at sonic speed—that would have been a very low priority scheme. Even with an airlock in place on Rigel's quarters. One miscalculation and all upon the *Onyx* could have perished. Morgana is eccentric, but not suicidal. Besides, she was fully vetted for this mission. *By me.* It wasn't her."

"We'll grant you that instinctive assessment, and move on. How about you? *You* had access to that room."

"I think I would know if I did it."

"I can assure you, given my abilities, that statement is not necessarily true."

"It wasn't me," Mary replied.

"Then I will indulge that assumption, as well. Proceed. What of Rigel herself? She could be acting out. Or making it look as if Earth was incapable of providing adequate protection for her."

"She was appropriately obnoxious when I pulled her out of that room. She had no idea."

"Alright. Bad manners as an alibi. Stranger things have served as evidence in the universe."

"There was only one other person who did have access to that room, even when Rigel wasn't in it. *Oirin.* And he was very desirous of a public procession upon Rigel's arrival on Lough Derg, an event which would have placed her in danger. He also seemed very anxious to know about Rigel's condition—*and if her quarters had been compromised*—when the possible compromise of her quarters was not knowledge available to him at the time. In addition, he served Rigel and Torin for over a decade. I suspect he served Torin alone. That he was an agent placed aboard the *Onyx* by Torin, with the mission of orchestrating an unfortunate accident for the exiled Queen Mother."

"You forgot to mention that Oirin was present—and completely ineffective—during the previous assassination attempt of Rigel's life while she was on Sri'Quis."

"I was going to add that next."

"Asset protection. What a dreary assignment you've drawn, Cecil. You are there to take a bullet for some cantankerous old biddy. And when she dies—of natural causes, for I am sure you will keep her alive—you will have no one left to take a bullet for. That must be a devastating moment. And *you* are pledged to protect someone you don't even like."

"My service does not depend on my affections."

"You do know that Rigel did not have her husband killed, correct?"

"She asserted so."

"Rigel is actually a very reliable woman and ruler. And she despises our mutual enemy, the Uoy. Which commends her to Earth. Dorhath, by contrast, was on the verge of signing an alliance with the Uoy. Torin is likewise a Uoy sympathizer. Earth—let us say that Earth was not at all saddened by Dorhath's untimely passing. Nor is Earth upset by Rigel's very legitimate claim to the Sri'Quisian throne. Earth is content to let Torin squirm for now, knowing that his mother has substantial support for her claim to his throne. *O me, with what strict patience have I sat, to see a king transformed to a gnat!*"

"*Love's Labor's Lost*, Act IV. Scene III," Mary observed. "Your knowledge of Shakespeare is impressive, considering that your dual doctorates are in forensic medicine and the culinary arts." She paused. "I suppose Earth has plausible deniability with regards to Dorhath's passing."

"Torin is an ambitious young man," Aize'Rcul replied. "Perhaps Torin desired to accelerate his father's mortality so that he himself would become king?"

"Torin fears he may find himself to be the next monarch who perishes unexpectedly in his sleep."

"He has lost his soul for his crown; he now rightfully fears that he may lose his life for it, as well," Aize'Rcul noted.

"Sri'Quisian Royal Family intrigue notwithstanding, I have a situation. Oirin will try to kill Rigel again. It is my duty to prevent that. However, Rigel trusts Oirin implicitly and he is the only one here she has known for decades. She will defend him and protect him. That makes my job more difficult to perform."

"I think you will find your problem already solved," Aize'Rcul comforted. "Oirin uses an imported wax to make that bald head of his shine. He claims that his shiny dome slays the ladies. He'll be partially validated. About the slaying part, at least. I think he is about to discover that his grooming regime will be the death of him."

"Is there no place safe from you?" Mary asked. "We don't even know where you are, yet you can eliminate this threat?"

"How could any calamity on Lough Derg possibly be ascribed to me? *I'm just a pirate*, Special Agent Cecil. Just as you are merely a bodyguard. Both of us worthy of trust and confidence, in our own ways." Mary could hear the sly smile on Dr. Ursula Manning's lips. It sent a chill up her spine.

"Enjoy your tour on Lough Derg," Aize'Rcul continued, "I always like the fresh cod they fish from the deep blue ocean there. The local chefs serve it with a delicious savory sauce containing just the right amount of Meyer lemon juice. The lemons are grown from Earth stock, on the western end of the Patrician Island. And you really should sit by the water's edge on the south-western edge of the Patrician Palace grounds. It is very soothing to the mind. And the position gives you a commanding view across the bay at the one and only road leading onto the palace grounds. By the way, do check the last two windows flanking the great hall in the palace itself—the ones on the left. You will find that they appear locked and armed, but have been rigged to be opened without setting off any alarms."

Aize'Rcul closed down the communication unceremoniously.

Mary Osprey looked out of her windows, gazing over the glorious deep blue waters of Lough Derg, noting that one lonely road that led to the palace grounds. She sensed their isolation—and their vulnerability—in this exile. She was on a planet, deep in country, waiting to deflect any implement of possible harm aimed towards an old woman who had once been queen.

And most likely would be again.

Mary considered that the cold vacuum of space seemed so much safer than the solid ground of Lough Derg.

The palace alarms were activated.

Undoubtedly, Oirin's body had been found.

"And now, Lady Rigel, it is just you and me," Mary thought. "But rest assured, I will serve unwaveringly."

Gald

Allyson Shaw

Call me Minnie, short for Minnesota, a place I've never been. It's just a name my mother saw on a map and took a liking too, or so the story goes. My mother gave me away when I was a bairn so I never knew her. Shasta took me. She was born of Janice, who worked at the fairs and taught Shasta the reading-show. You tell a stranger something they know about themselves and something they don't, and they pay you for it. Janice died in the riots, and she was daughter to Annalise who lived a very long time and died in a bed.

We are all illegal, no profiles, no scan codes, no fish tickets, nothing. Shasta said she once had her irises printed, though she fought like a wild cat and they had to hold her down to do it. "What did the big eye see when it looked in?" I had asked her. She made her eyes bulge out, "All my secrets!" and laughed but I could tell this dogged her, that they took a bit of her when they did it.

There's Raynald with us. Shasta calls him the Highland branch of the family. His father's father was a pearl fisherman, back when there were mussels in the rivers. He is old now, but still has a pearls in his pockets. He says our people go back to the Painted Ones that etched their wyrd in the skin with woad. They carved the great stones and some of them are still standing. We make our way by those stones sometimes, carved with the long-nosed beasts that look like the dolphins that swim in groups come spring, flying up from the water in taut arcs. Our people knew the beasts well, Raynald said, and the beasts knew them.

Sometimes you wonder why you are the only ones left, but then the gull chicks wake you up early, and you are so happy for the salt air and the dumplings Shasta's boiling over the fire, you forget to think any more about it. Shasta held out hope that we weren't the only ones, and some day we'd find others. That's why I had to learn the language, so they would know me as kin if they ever found us.

In high summer you can walk all day and food is everywhere. But in the winter, you bed down in an empty barn or abandoned golf course, now gone wild with seed, and you wouldn't be above eating a feral dog or one of the cats from the cliffside colonies if the rabbits were scarce.

I watched Shasta shake the jar of yarrow flowers and whisky and chant as she did every morning. "Word follows word—I was given these words. Work follows work. I was given this work."

With her eyes closed and throat high, she sang the oldest words over them, just three that she said the plant had given her when she cut it. She called that singing gald. Shasta had a box of jars that she kept hidden under the provisions, and under the jars were the vials, the lixirs Shasta made only at the blood moon, working in secret so that even I didn't know how she did it. They were wrapped in velvet cloths embroidered with the words, which were also letters, pictures that I had only just learned to write. Lixirs can do many things. They can break a fever, mend a wound, but then lots of things can that aren't so hard to make. They can make you forget, and every single one can kill you if you take it wrong, but that could also be said about many things. It can help a bairn find its way to this world, or the next, as the case may be. But there was one that did something else, something Shasta never mentioned in all our lessons. I asked her about it.

"This," she said holding up the little glass bottle filled with milky blue liquid with its ornate blue filigree around the stopper, "is on a need-to-know basis."

We were our own country, the three of us with our horse and the old sedan, the cart with three wheels that we pulled Shasta in. Raynald was older than any of us and remembered a time when it was all one place, not a bunch of little sokes, each with a lord that needed appeasing if we were to pass through conspicuous-like.

We stayed in a tower block inside a soke, once upon a time, or so Shasta says. I can't remember that far back.

You wouldn't go near one now, of course, but back then, she says, we all stayed inside them, back before the blackouts, the shortages and the riots, before the Guard came. I only remember walking. Shasta has many summers on me and I have to take her word.

We stick to the old corpse roads, the tracks what were walked before the cameras and bypasses. You go north enough you can track your way by the wind turbines, the water on your right if you are going west, which we were.

We mostly travelled at night, setting up camp in dense woods or disused industrial parks like the one we were in now. Raynald says it used to be grassland where he camped with his father. Things still grew wild through the tarmac and verges, if you knew what to look for, as Shasta did.

"Look at them poppies!" she said, showing me their tender necks nodding beside the razor wire fence. They were brilliant red like some pretty dress torn to shreds. We made a note to come back at the next fat moon to get the little star-topped lanterns full of seeds.

There was always plenty of hegbeg. I hated the sting, gathering it. Sneaking up on it unawares didn't help. Showing it who was boss (Shasta's tip) didn't help either. I wasn't anyone's boss.

This twilight, I was out getting the hegbeg for stewing up. It was past it for the lixir, but it was still good to eat.

We had a stove set up outside with the pot simmering with the hegbeg, bitter tooth, and a handful of beans when the lady came. Raynald had set up the tents, one for Shasta and me, another for him. We warmed ourselves around the fire, its brightness making the dusk duskier. That's when I saw her. Who walks out in a white dress like that, like a surrender flag?

As she came closer, I thought she must smell the soup and want some. I elbowed Shasta who'd nodded off. The lady was close enough that I could see her haunted eyes, her mincing step over the tall grass.

We all watched her coming, but Raynald got up. Old as he was, he was still a big man. The woman hesitated, like a doe that's heard the hunter's step.

"How did she get out of the sokes?" Shasta wondered.

"What if she were followed?" Raynald worried. "If she's led the drones to us..."

All that pale hair tangled with little twigs and flowers and the dirt on her face made her look like a fairy woman. My eyes adjusted to the half light, and I could see her little belly starting to round out when the rest of her was thin as anything.

"Didn't anyone take a mercy on you, Ray?" Shasta must have seen it too. "Sit down," she hissed and stood up slow, beckoning the woman to come. Why she did that, we'll never know. Too kind hearted, she was.

We didn't ask her anything, just watched her drink a big mug of steaming beg tea with a drop of whisky and some much prized sugar in it, our blanket about her shoulders. She drank the tea so fast, she probably burned her mouth. She said, "My name is Venlis, of the Machar Soke." Though she held out her hand, none of us took it.

"You best think of a new name, now." Shasta spread out the silk on the little collapsible table for the reading-show, ready to make a map of the old words. Venlis put her trembling hand in Shasta's old one and watched it like it wasn't her hand at all and might do something terrible.

"What do you see?" Venlis asked, as if she'd had a reading-show before and it was something you asked people like Shasta, like us.

"Everybody's got the same hand," Shasta said, which is what she always said, because she didn't read lines on a palm. That was beneath her. She shook the bag of marked stones and shells, and asked the woman to pull three. She told me for real power, you can't use the words, their symbols, pulled out of the bag like raisins from a cake, but you can ask a stranger to do it that way, the same way a plant might give you three to gald over it. The words sing the long story of the world, from beginning to end, and can't be interrupted, but a stranger could take three as a test.

"Silence I ask from the kin, living and dead. If it please the Hanged One, I will speak of things forgot, for I am the far-seeing one wise in wyrd." When she would say those words, we all hushed.

I never seen a one so scared as this Venlis. Everything she wore was delicate, shimmering, not made to last a day. Her face was painted, with blue clouds around her eyes, smearing down her cheeks, and her lips peeling dark red paint. She had jewels on her hands, sparkling in the firelight. No doubt those would be coming with us. But where would she go? I wondered. She reached into the bag with certainty, as if the things inside were money she were counting, and pulled out three etched shells.

Shasta laid them out, the corners of her mouth turning down, hard.

The woman could see it too. "No..." she said and started to cry.

"You went out to find a place to curl up and die, and it turns out you don't die so easy." That, Venlis knew. She snuffled, wiped her nose with the back of her wrist, "But?" she guessed.

"But now you are stuck, with nowhere to go." This she also knew.

"What can I do? Can I come with you?"

Raynald sucked his teeth and Shasta shushed him.

"You come with us as far as Groats, where there is a man with a boat who can help you." This was news to her, what the strangers pay for. Venlis steeled herself to the idea and sat up straight.

Raynald was so cross, he just got up and walked away from the camp. We fell asleep waiting for him to come back. We all slept together, huddled-like in the tent. When I heard Venlis snoring, I liked her better.

I woke to Raynald's shaking me. "The drones are coming in." He went straight for the lixirs, and I woke Shasta and the lady.

We ran, though not fast because Shasta was slow. Their buzzing bore down on us. Raynald half-dragged, half-carried Shasta and we took cover in a big empty shed, halfway to the sea.

"I brought them, didn't I?" Venlis was crying again.

Shasta fumbled with the box of vials and brought out the milky blue one. She made me and Venlis take a sip. It was bitter, like biting down on metal, and scored your insides going down.

"Go to the sea. Run," Shasta urged. We were fast, even with the lixir in our bellies, changing us, maybe because of it. Venlis screeched to bring them after us, away from Shasta and Raynald. We tumbled down the cliffside, the drones whirring nearby.

Splash, into the cold water we went, all dressed. We swam but already the lights were dimming in our heads, the drones skimming the water to scan us. I could see a cave up ahead, at the base of the cliffs. The drones crunched and clicked, whizzing up their guns, their tiny boxes talking and dreaming small, bright pictures.

We crawled into a cave, the ceiling all decorated with tiny skulls hanging, clacking together in the wind. The sea was coming up now, the tide coming in with a quick certainty.

This cave! All glittering with pieces of bright stone, the words singing the story of the world carved there. I could barely see the drones anymore, hovering over the frothing water that might drag us out with its cold hands. Venlis was dimming so that all that was left were the glowing shapes on the walls. She smiled at me, breathless and exhilarated, changed to a slick beast. She opened her long muzzle, trilled and whistled. My own buzzing bounced off her and we swam.

THANK YOU TO OUR SUPPORTERS

Many thanks to our patrons and supporters, especially:

Johanna Levene • Stephanie Johnston
Anna O'Brien • Cathrin Hagey
S Naomi Scott • Natalie Weizenbaum
Siobhan Beeman

Emily Anderson • Felicia OSullivan • J'nae Spano
Katherine Montalto • Kennon Hulett • Katie Conrad
Martin Cohen • Salomao Becker • Anne Worth
Shannon White • Tamara Rutledge • Tory Hoke
Bonnie Warford • Kara • Frederick Stark • Kel • Wanda
Erik DeBill • BethOfAus • Aidan Long • Carol Shoemake

Brit Hvide • Carly Racklin • Charlotte Nash-Stewart
Dirck de Lint • GriffinFire • J Askew
Jocelyn Actual • Karen Anderson
Jen G • Kayla • Liz Warner • Ally Shaw
Maria Haskins • Suzanne Thackston

Want to see your name here? Become a patron!
patreon.com/lunastation

About the Cover Artist

Anna is an illustrator and concept artist working with various international clients and publishers such as Wizards of the Coast, Games Workshop, Ulisses Spiele, Simon&Schuster and more.

Her free time is devoted her own passion project Veritas, an illustrated storybook set in a whimsical world of witches, magic and mystery. You can get early access to the art, as well as insight into Anna's creative process by becoming a patron on Patreon.

You can find more of her work at:

www.annasteinbauer.com

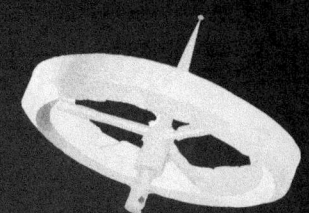

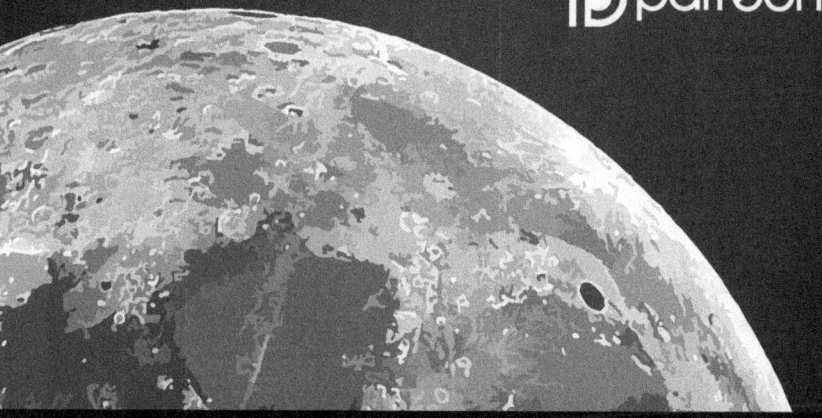